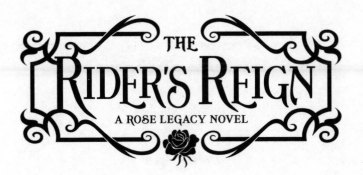

THE RIDER'S REIGN

A ROSE LEGACY NOVEL

Also by Jessica Day George

Dragon Slippers
Dragon Flight
Dragon Spear

~⚬~

Tuesdays at the Castle
Wednesdays in the Tower
Thursdays with the Crown
Fridays with the Wizards
Saturdays at Sea

~⚬~

Sun and Moon, Ice and Snow

~⚬~

Princess of the Midnight Ball
Princess of Glass
Princess of the Silver Woods

~⚬~

Silver in the Blood

~⚬~

The Rose Legacy
The Queen's Secret

THE RIDER'S REIGN

A ROSE LEGACY NOVEL

Jessica Day George

BLOOMSBURY
CHILDREN'S BOOKS
NEW YORK   LONDON   OXFORD   NEW DELHI   SYDNEY

BLOOMSBURY CHILDREN'S BOOKS
Bloomsbury Publishing Inc., part of Bloomsbury Publishing Plc
1385 Broadway, New York, NY 10018

BLOOMSBURY, BLOOMSBURY CHILDREN'S BOOKS, and the Diana logo
are trademarks of Bloomsbury Publishing Plc

First published in the United States of America in June 2020
by Bloomsbury Children's Books

Bloomsbury books may be purchased for business or promotional use. For information on
bulk purchases please contact Macmillan Corporate and Premium Sales Department at
specialmarkets@macmillan.com

Library of Congress Cataloging-in-Publication Data
Names: George, Jessica Day, author.
Title: The rider's reign / by Jessica Day George.
Description: New York : Bloomsbury Children's Books, 2020. |
Series: [Rose legacy ; book 3]
Summary: Anthea gathers her friends to meet with the antagonistic emperor
of Kronenhof, hoping to find Coronami princess Margaret, the herd stallion,
and other horses her mother has taken before war breaks out.
Identifiers: LCCN 2020002355 (print) | LCCN 2020002356 (e-book)
ISBN 978-1-5476-0121-9 (hardcover) • ISBN 978-1-5476-0122-6 (e-book)
Subjects: CYAC: Fantasy. | Human-animal communication—Fiction. | Horses—Fiction.
Classification: LCC PZ7.G293317 Rid 2020 (print) | LCC PZ7.G293317 (e-book) |
DDC [Fic]—dc23
LC record available at https://lccn.loc.gov/2020002355

Book design by John Candell
Typeset by Westchester Publishing Services
Printed and bound in the U.S.A. by Berryville Graphics Inc., Berryville, Virginia
2 4 6 8 10 9 7 5 3 1

To find out more about our authors and books visit www.bloomsbury.com
and sign up for our newsletters.

This one's for my whole family:

The outlaws, the in-laws,

The clever cousins, mustachioed uncles, and favorite aunts,

The adorable and hilarious nieces and nephews,

I love you all!

THE RIDER'S REIGN

A ROSE LEGACY NOVEL

The Battle Begins

"YOU'VE BEEN PREPARING FOR battle all your life," Anthea whispered. "Why are you nervous?"

"Battle? This isn't battle!" Jilly's whisper was too shrill, and the man in line in front of them turned around to glare.

He turned back quickly as the enormous oak doors—inlaid with the Kronenhofer Royal Crest in gold—opened. A footman looked at the man with raised eyebrows, and the man stalked out, straightening his coat. The doors closed behind him, and Jilly gulped audibly.

"Of course this is battle," Anthea said. "Haven't you been paying attention?"

"You've done your best, Anthea," Jilly's mother, Lady Cassandra, said, fussing around them with light fingers. "But there really is no substitute for Rose Academy training." She stepped back, frowned at her daughter, and then turned to Anthea with a smile. "Miss Miniver's touch is unmistakable," she said with approval as she looked over her niece.

"Ahem," Jilly said pointedly. "You said I was—"

"Ready?" Finn asked. He looked as nervous as Jilly.

"It's *just* a battle, it's just a *battle*," Jilly whispered.

"The *drama*," Lady Cassandra said, rolling her eyes. She gave Finn a little push. "*You* know what to do!"

Finn threw back his shoulders, holding out his elbows for Anthea and Jilly. The doors opened. Anthea's stomach dropped to her shoes.

"The Lord of Leana, Finn magTaran," the footman's voice boomed in Anthea's ear, and she would have shied like a horse without Finn there to keep her steady. "The Lady Anthea Cross-Thornley, and the Lady Jillian Thornley."

Anthea froze at the sound of her name. *Not Cross*, she wanted to whisper to the man. *Only Thornley*. But he had gone on, oblivious to her distress.

"The Lady Cassandra Locke," he announced.

They entered a glittering ballroom, with crystal chandeliers throwing prisms against the gilded walls. The mellow wood of the floor was so highly polished that it, too, looked like gold. Or at least what you could see of it looked like gold. The room was so full of people that it was difficult to see anything except the black of the men's suits and the swirling colors of the women's gowns, plumes bobbing above their heads, jewels flashing.

And every eye was on Anthea and her companions.

"We're breathing, we're doing this, we're fine," Finn said without moving his lips.

They started down the shallow stairs to the ballroom floor, with Anthea's gold gauze overdress floating around her raspberry pink silk slip.

During their journey from Travertine to Kronenhof, Lady Cassandra had gone through all their things and threatened to throw the bulk of them overboard. Jilly and Anthea had prevented that (mostly), but the compromise was to allow Lady Cassandra and her maid to alter their gowns, and to fit them out with some she had brought with her.

Anthea was quite pleased with her new wardrobe. She had intended on wearing her white silk gown with the red roses to this first court function, but when Jilly and Lady Cassandra pointed out that it made her look a great deal like her own mother, Anthea had thrown it overboard herself.

Jilly's gown was a bit more avant-garde than Anthea's. There were several layers of different fabrics in varying shades of green, and the skirt was all different lengths . . . some of them scandalously short. Her shoes had green ribbons that crisscrossed all the way up her legs to the knee, and she wore a ring on every finger. When Lady Cassandra had opened her mouth to demand that her daughter change, Jilly had merely arched an eyebrow.

"The queen told us to make a splash, milady," she had said,

her voice as cool as it always was when speaking to Cassandra, whom she refused to call "Mother."

To balance out the splash Jilly was making, Anthea and Finn were dressed in the latest and most correct fashions. Anthea's gown was the newest cut from Travertine, and Finn looked very uncomfortable in a stiff black tuxedo. He had tried to wear the formal kilt and jacket he had brought from home, but Lady Cassandra had screamed in feigned horror at the thought of him "parading about like a barbarian with his legs on display."

She did, however, recommend that he keep his kilt and jacket pressed and ready because there was a "time and place for that sort of thing." Neither Jilly nor Anthea had yet learned what that time and place might be, but Anthea, for one, was very curious.

They passed between the dancers, who had stopped moving to watch them. Anthea tried to walk gracefully, but with confidence, as they headed toward the dais on the far side of the room. Jilly, naturally, let her silver heels strike the floor in time to the music that was still playing despite the disinterest in dancing. Anthea knew that Jilly was nervous, but a nervous Jilly was much more likely to be outrageous. Lady Cassandra, despite having been absent from her daughter's life since Jilly was a baby, seemed to know it, too.

"Just keep walking and smiling," came the whisper from behind them. "Walking and smiling!"

At last they reached the dais. Anthea felt a rush of relief pass through her when she saw who was on it. Or rather, who *wasn't* on it. Her mother was nowhere to be seen, and for that Anthea sent up a little prayer of gratitude.

In the three days since they had arrived in Kronenhof, they had mostly sat in the beautiful suite they had been given, finishing their new wardrobes in between going down to the hastily cleaned garden shed where their horses were being kept. When Anthea had first heard that the emperor had designated a shed for their use, she had been highly offended, and also baffled that the Kronenhofer thought you could keep five large animals in a shed at all.

But then she had seen the palace, or *schloss*, or fortress, or whatever the emperor wanted to call it. Queen Josephine's beloved Bell Hyde would fit in the Empress's Wing of Schloss Kronen. The gardens went on for miles and even contained fake ruins where the old emperor had kept a couple of elderly servants who posed as mad wizards to entertain guests. This garden shed was very nearly the size of the stable at the Last Farm.

Bringing her mind back to the present before people noticed her woolgathering, Anthea let go of Finn's arm and curtsied. Out of the corner of her eye, she saw Finn bow and Jilly curtsy. She kept her knees bent and her eyes lowered until she heard the emperor's gruff command to "Rise!"

She thought he made them stay down just a hair too long.

Miss Miniver had warned her about this; according to the headmistress it was something weak leaders did to prove their power.

She put on exactly the degree of smile that Miss Miniver thought appropriate when greeting someone you disliked but who was nonetheless higher ranking. Jilly would have scoffed at such information being called "education" . . . in point of fact, Anthea had rather thought it useless at the time herself. But now here they were, and Miss Miniver's schooling was just what was needed.

Anthea kept her eyes demurely lowered and used the concealment of her tastefully darkened lashes to observe the emperor and his family. In the meantime, Lady Cassandra made her curtsy and reminded the emperor of the summer she had spent at his court with the old queen, King Gareth's mother, Juliane.

Emperor Wilhelm the Third of Kronenhof was an imposing man. Tall and broad-shouldered, he had been lauded for his heroics in the Bremeni uprising in his youth, and he had kept up a soldier's regimen. His thick chest was muscular beneath his heavily decorated coat, and his scarlet sash was tied around a trim waist. Over the sash was a sword belt—not an ornamental one, but a well-oiled and well-worn belt, from which hung an equally serviceable scabbard holding a heavy saber. As was the Kronenhof custom, he wore no crown, which showed to advantage his thick, wavy iron-gray hair.

Finn made a brief speech about how generous the emperor had been in making them feel welcome. He thanked him for the accommodations for their horses, and invited the emperor to meet the horses at his earliest convenience.

While this was happening, Anthea stole a look at the rest of the group on the dais. There was just one woman, a tall ivory-skinned blonde barely older than Anthea—Princess Wilhelmina, the only daughter of Emperor Wilhelm. She wore a blue gown draped with an overdress of ivory lace that Anthea was certain was antique . . . worth more than the pearls around the princess's neck and dangling from her ears.

There were two others on the dais, young men in dress uniforms with nearly as many medals as the emperor. Neither of them looked old enough to be in the army at all, let alone have achieved such honors. Anthea knew that the emperor had a son her age, the Imperial Crown Prince Fritz, and guessed from his pale coloring, similar to Wilhelmina's, that he was the young man on the emperor's left. The other, standing slightly behind the others, was the one who really piqued her curiosity. Because, although he wore the same green uniform as the prince and they were much the same height, he was plainly Kadiji, with even darker skin and more tightly curled hair than Anthea's friend Keth . . . but then, Keth's mother was Leanan.

The emperor had long been dangling the idea of an alliance between his son and one of the Coronami princesses;

Anthea supposed he had done the same thing with countries with eligible princes for his daughter. But if the young Kadiji was there to court Princess Wilhelmina, why was he wearing a Kronenhofer uniform?

Lady Cassandra was done introducing them, and Finn was done thanking the emperor for his hospitality both for their people and their horses. The mention of the horses made everyone on the dais perk up.

"I must confess I've taken a peep at them," the Imperial Heir said. "Enormous beasts! So bizarre that you sit on them!"

"I'd rather die," Princess Wilhelmina drawled. "They probably get hair and dirt all over your gowns." She raked Anthea and Jilly with her eyes, pointedly checking their skirts for filth.

"We don't wear gowns when we ride," Jilly drawled right back. "Trousers are *so* much more convenient."

There were gasps from the ladies standing nearby to eavesdrop. Anthea had been worried that no one at the court would speak Coronami. She had studied Kronenhofer, but read it more fluently than she spoke it. That wouldn't be a problem, it seemed. Besides which, the emperor barely had an accent. His children sounded as though they had been raised in Travertine.

"I would *love* to see you ride, Lady Jillian," the prince said. He didn't look like he thought she had filth on her skirts.

"We will all watch you ride," the emperor said. "We will all admire your horses and witness your bond with them."

The princess snorted.

"Silly fairy tales," she muttered in Kronenhofer.

The emperor raised a hand, silencing her. The princess sulked, and gave Anthea a glare as though she were at fault.

"We will visit you and your beasts tomorrow morning," he announced. "You may enjoy yourselves now."

Dismissed, Anthea turned away from the dais. Plenty of guests were still staring at them, but the music hadn't stopped and people were dancing again. Finn led them to one of the small tables, and Lady Cassandra sat down.

"That went very well," she said. She nodded in satisfaction. "Now—"

"I'm going to get food," Jilly said.

"I was too nervous to eat before," Finn admitted. "But I'm starving."

"Jillian," Lady Cassandra began.

"Don't worry, I'll get enough for the whole table," Jilly said, and left.

Anthea moved to sit when Lady Cassandra said, "Don't be ridiculous. You must dance."

Anthea looked around.

"With Finn," Lady Cassandra said with a sigh. "But remember, should anyone else ask you . . . ?"

"I must dance with them or sit out the rest of the night," Anthea recited.

"What, really?" Finn said. "What if he's . . . I don't know . . . a murderer or something?"

"Murderers don't attend balls," Lady Cassandra said severely.

"Shall we?"

Lady Cassandra had said "murderers" a trifle too loudly. Chaperones at the nearby tables were turning to look. Anthea quickly led Finn onto the dance floor.

"I know how to dance," Finn muttered.

"You do *now*," Anthea said.

She was trying to joke, but it came out too sharp. They had spent hours on the boat learning to dance—well, Anthea already knew how, and had been enlisted by Lady Cassandra to teach Finn and Jilly. Jilly was prone to throwing in her own steps and wild arm movements. Finn was a quick learner, but he couldn't seem to get rid of the strained expression on his face.

Anthea was still so nervous, and because Finn looked to be in actual pain as he led her into the figures of the dance, she burst out laughing.

Finn froze, but Anthea kept him moving. His surprise kept her laughing, although much more demurely. One benefit was that it changed his expression from wooden intensity to mere confusion.

She let out another little giggle. "It's just . . . your face!"

"I can't help it!" Finn said through gritted teeth that almost looked like a smile. "I have this fear that if I lose count or turn the wrong way, they'll have me killed!"

"Who will?"

"Lady Cassandra, for starters!"

Anthea laughed outright again. Finn expertly swung her around the couple on their left, and they began the long promenade down the middle of the floor, with the other dancers lined up on each side, clapping in time.

"See!" Anthea spoke out of the corner of her mouth. "You can do this!"

"Did you sneak some champagne?"

"I didn't," Anthea said, her smile fading in indignation. "I think I'm just giddy!"

"From the dancing?"

Anthea felt a hot flush rise up her cheeks. They were standing across from each other now, waiting for the next couple to make their way down the line. Finn could clearly see her blush, and she could hardly shout across to him that it wasn't his hands holding hers that was causing her to blush.

They finally rejoined and moved into smaller eight-hand circles, and Anthea could explain. Her blush had faded by then, fortunately.

"I'm just happy because we did it," Anthea said. "We met the emperor! He wants us to show him our horses! That's all good news, right?"

"We still have to pretend that he doesn't know about

horses, and doesn't know your mother," Finn whispered when the dance allowed them to move closer together.

"And pretend they didn't kidnap Meg," Anthea agreed, her smile fading further.

They had spent the journey, when not practicing dances or being fitted for new clothes, rehearsing their story about Princess Margaret. Anthea's mother, Genevia, had kidnapped Meg and half a dozen horses, destroying a village in the process. Even worse: one of the horses was Constantine, the herd stallion and king of the horses. They suspected that Genevia had made a deal with the emperor, who had supplied her with soldiers and a monstrous machine called a schutzer-something— an armored car with an enormous gun mounted on the front.

In order to avoid a war, Anthea and her companions had to pretend they knew nothing of this, and to find Meg and the horses as quickly and quietly as possible. The official word from Coronam was that Meg had gone on a holiday with some feckless friends, and Lady Cassandra, Jilly, and Anthea were being sent as belated chaperones. Finn was originally to be their bodyguard, but the moment he had set foot on Kronenhofer soil, the emissary from the emperor had given Finn the title "Lord of Leana."

So now he was an ambassador from his "cousin" Queen Josephine. They were likely distantly related, but neither the queen nor Finn knew how. Fortunately, no one had asked yet. In fact, they had barely spoken to anyone at all.

The servants came and went silently, bringing clean towels and trays of food, and demonstrating the ornate bathroom taps. Groundskeepers showed them where to put the horses. A footman came with a tray bearing the invitation to this ball, but like the others he said nothing. It was eerie how silent they were, how stone-faced.

It was going to be a lot harder to find Meg if no one would talk to them.

"We'll need to make a good impression on His Imperial Highness tomorrow," Anthea said. "We need to show him our bond with the horses, as well as how intelligent they are."

"Do you think he's met Constantine?" Finn asked. "He must have known your mother's plan. He could be hiding the stolen horses and Meg right here. Schloss Kronen is his principal residence; he never travels unless he absolutely has to."

It was a discussion they had had many times in the past few days.

"Impossible," Anthea said. "We would know if they were nearby! We would feel them, be able to speak to them!" She paused, and then they continued toward Lady Cassandra and their seats. "I don't think he has ever seen a horse. No one here has. But there was something about their faces . . ."

She wanted to think that her mother had acted alone, horrible as that sounded. She didn't want to cause a war, or have to fight an *emperor* to get Constantine back.

When the king retired for the night, giving the guests

permission to also seek their beds, Anthea sighed in relief. They had all played their parts well, but it hadn't been easy. She felt like she had been on a hard ride, and that made her want to check on Florian, but since the hour had drawn quite late it would have to wait until morning.

As she started to make her way to her room, arm in arm with Jilly while Finn trailed behind them, Lady Cassandra suddenly flew at them from behind a marble statue of some Kronenhofer ancestor. She pulled them into a quiet corner, a piece of paper fluttering in one white hand.

"Whoa, where's the fire?" Jilly asked, yawning.

Lady Cassandra's face was drawn and serious. "I went to check on my dogs," she said, breathless. "And when I got to my room I found this!" She held up the paper. "We've received a letter from the queen. We only have two weeks."

She paused to breathe, so Anthea said, "Two weeks until what?"

"If the Crown hasn't heard from Meg in two weeks, they're going to declare war with Kronenhof."

UNWELCOME LETTER

"*WAR?*" JILLY EXCLAIMED, so loudly that a passing gentleman turned to look. Lady Cassandra hissed in displeasure. "Does the letter really say that?" Jilly asked, her voice much quieter.

Anthea's mind was racing. Two weeks was not a lot of time at all. She blinked rapidly, trying to think, when a horrifying thought entered her mind. "Wait, *when* was that letter sent? Is the deadline two weeks from *today* or two weeks from when it was posted?"

Lady Cassandra simply held the paper out for Anthea to take. Jilly looked over Anthea's shoulder.

Anthea couldn't help but feel a pang of jealousy that the queen had written to Lady Cassandra and not to her. Or even to Jilly. They were, after all, Her Majesty's Horse Maidens. Surely that warranted a separate letter?

But then she saw the heading, and all was forgiven.

Dear Cassandra and also My Dear Girls!
I addressed the envelope to Cassandra, because I
felt that a letter to one of my Rose Maidens was less
likely to be intercepted. I am sure that someone will still
read this, but at least it will then make its way to you!

"Oh, my!" Jilly exclaimed. "She just came right out and
said that? Our Josie is so fabulous!"

"And so brave," Anthea murmured.

But she felt a little frightened. It worried her to have the
queen challenging people in that way. They had left Coronam
on the eve of the queen's announcement that she was Leanan,
and they still weren't sure how her husband, the king, would
feel about that.

I wanted you to know that my husband, Gareth,
has been in talks with the emperor. We are all very
concerned that Meg has not written to us about her
travels, as promised, and we are most eager to hear
from her. The king, my husband, has told Emperor
Wilhelm that if we have not heard from Meg in two
weeks (as of the first of the month), then he will be
sending over some of his men to look for her very
aggressively.

I am sending you all my best thoughts and
affection.

Yours,

Josephine

"The first was yesterday," Finn said.

Anthea said, "I'm relieved that she got this letter to us so fast . . . but two weeks!"

"Wait, she didn't actually *say* that they would declare war against Kronenhof . . . right?" Jilly asked.

"No," her mother responded, "but she can't very well say that outright. The meaning, however, is quite clear."

Anthea looked at the letter again, while Finn and Jilly nodded solemnly. Anthea felt the blood draining from her face and pooling in her feet. Her stomach went wobbly.

A war. And they were on foreign, hostile, soil. What was that saying? About spies?

"Trapped behind enemy lines," she muttered.

"We'll just have to hurry—" Jilly began.

"Yes," Lady Cassandra agreed. "We have a lot of work to do, so we best be off to get a good night's sleep."

Finn turned to walk with Anthea, murmuring, "Things will be better in the morning. Once the emperor meets Florian and the others, he'll be moved. I know he will."

Anthea nodded, letting out a breath she didn't realize she was holding. At least things couldn't get any worse.

Beloved, Florian said to her through the Way. Sensing her anxiety about the letter, he had been listening in.

Yes, my love?

I have already met this Bearded Imperial Highness.

What?

He has come every day to the stable when you are not here.

Why didn't you tell me?

I did not want to frighten you, Beloved, Florian said humbly. *He smells of dead roses. We do not like him.*

3

THIS BEARDED
IMPERIAL HIGHNESS

ANTHEA DRESSED AND WENT to the stables at dawn the next morning. She did not enjoy mornings. Even after months of waking before dawn to care for a dozen horses when the Dag struck many of the riders, Anthea still struggled. Jilly and Finn usually avoided talking to her for her first hour awake, and she appreciated that.

She got to the stable just as dawn was peeking over the tall trees of the imperial park, pulling her heavy gray army coat close over her delicate silk blouse and straightening her Horse Maiden pin—a gold rosebud cupped by a horse-shoe—to the lapel. Within moments, the emperor arrived with his attendants: the disdainful Princess Wilhelmina, a pair of guards, and the dashing Prince Fritz.

Groggy, Anthea just stared at them until the emperor finally spoke.

"I'm sure it is difficult to curtsy in trousers," he growled.

"What? Oh!"

Anthea gave a little bob that was not quite curtsy, not quite bow, but seemed to mollify the emperor. He was already looking beyond her at the door of the stable, but those with him looked at her with varying expressions of amusement or disgust.

"Halloooo!"

Just as they were going into the stable, with Anthea holding the door for them all, including the guards, Jilly ran toward them. She wore tight trousers, a bright blue cabled jumper, and a long pink silk scarf that trailed behind her, along with Finn, walking far more sedately. One of the guards put a hand to his pistol, and Anthea raised her scarred eyebrow.

"I wouldn't if I were you," she said. Inside the stable, Florian snorted loudly and scraped the floor with a hoof.

The guard swallowed and let his hand drop. Jilly arrived, delightfully rosy-cheeked and not at all out of breath. She favored them all with a dazzling smile.

"Shall we?"

Jilly pushed past the guards to step into the stable on the emperor's heels. Somehow she managed to displace Princess Wilhelmina and take Prince Fritz's arm before either of them knew what was happening.

"Oh, that's not going to be good," Finn whispered as he reached Anthea.

The expression on Princess Wilhelmina's face as Jilly swanned past her sent a shiver down Anthea's spine. Anthea and Finn hurried in before Jilly could make any more enemies.

"I haven't even had breakfast yet," Anthea muttered.

"I've got two scones in my pocket," Finn whispered.

That startled a bleat of laughter from Anthea. Everyone turned to look at her. Squaring her shoulders, she cleared her throat, smiled, and went over to the hastily constructed stall holding Florian.

Beloved, he greeted her. *Are you frightened? Who has frightened you?*

It is all right, she replied. *I just don't like it here.* A wave of homesickness overwhelmed her, and she hid her face in his mane.

"This is Florian," Finn said, standing a little in front of Anthea so that they couldn't see her face. "He is the herd stallion right now."

"Right now?" Emperor Wilhelm asked. "Is he an elected official?" He laughed at his own joke, and his people laughed with him.

"In a manner of speaking," Finn said stiffly. "He is the strongest stallion in this place. When we are at home, the herd stallion is Constantine, the largest and strongest of our entire herd."

"But this girl rides him, eh?"

The emperor pointed to Anthea, who had pulled herself

together and now was standing quietly at Florian's head, one hand on his neck. He needed to be groomed, but she felt it would be rude to turn her back on the emperor to brush her horse.

"Yes, this is Lady Anthea's horse, along with Leonidas"—he pointed to the darker stallion—"and the mare Bluebell." Finn gestured to her.

Bluebell put her gray head over the gate to her stall and looked at them, unimpressed. It had taken Anthea far longer to win Bluebell's respect than Florian's; the mare was notoriously standoffish.

Good morning, Anthea greeted her.

We have not been fed yet, and these intruders smell oddly, Bluebell retorted.

Anthea did her best not to smile or start laughing again. As the emperor moved down the aisle to meet the other horses, she hurried to get food for Florian and Bluebell, and then the other horses. Jilly and Finn stayed with the imperial family, while the guards took up positions on either side of the doorway.

Anthea was about to ask one of them to stop staring at her while she struggled with the huge barrel of oats and actually help, when Emperor Wilhelm's voice rang out addressing Finn.

"Why isn't your horse the herd stallion? What's wrong with him? Or is it wrong with you?"

"The strongest stallion, physically, is the herd stallion," Finn said again, his voice tight.

Anthea was pouring oats into a bucket for Leonidas. She stopped and grabbed hold of his black mane. He was not as close to her heart as Florian—no horse was—but since their adventure a year ago he was devoted to her, and she to him.

Once Leonidas had been known as a bold creature, difficult to ride, but having been injured (and seen Anthea injured) because of his mistakes had made him thoughtful and almost shy. He pressed his shoulder against her chest now, anxious. She put her arm over his back, holding him as well as she could.

"Marius was . . . hurt . . . recently," Finn said. "So Florian took charge."

Gentle Marius, who had never complained when Finn began to ride Constantine instead of him, had suffered from physical exhaustion and a nervous breakdown during the horrific abduction of Constantine and the other horses. Guilt-ridden, Finn had slept in the stable at his side on the journey to Kronenhof, but they all suspected that Marius would never be the same.

"What about this other herd stallion, this horse king, we have heard about?" Emperor Wilhelm flicked his gaze around the stable. He gave the appearance of looking for Constantine, but Anthea could tell that he knew Con wasn't here.

From the way his gaze didn't stop on any of the horses, she was willing to bet he knew exactly what Constantine looked like.

The real question: Did he know where Constantine was now?

I do not like him, Leonidas said.

She stroked the fine scars on Leonidas's black flank reassuringly. *Nor do I.*

"*Kron und Himmel!*" Princess Wilhelmina shrieked. "Vermin!"

Anthea vaulted over the gate to Leonidas's stall. The last thing they needed was an infestation of rats in the shed. They would spoil the horses' food, and the horses could get nasty infected bites.

But there were no rats. There was just one small creature, climbing out of a pile of straw—Arthur, Anthea's pet owl.

Anthea had brought him out to the stable last night before the ball, not wanting to leave him alone in her room. He was not fond of mornings, either, and now he had straw stuck in his feathers and a general air of irritation. He was a burrowing owl who flew in only short bursts, so Anthea knelt down and held out her hands for him to walk into. She plucked out the bits of straw before tucking him inside her coat, where she had sewn a large, soft pocket for him. When she looked up, the Kronenhofer party was staring at her. Beyond them, Finn looked amused.

"His name is Arthur," Anthea said.

Princess Wilhelmina looked as though she might be sick. But the emperor merely raised his eyebrows, and Prince Fritz, once he got over his shock, looked frankly impressed.

"What else do you have as pets?" he asked. "Horses, an owl . . . are there wolves and dragons hidden here, too?"

"Just the owl, and the horses," Jilly said. Her voice was cheerful, but there was an edge to it that Anthea recognized. "Not that I would say no to a wolf. Or a dragon." She smiled brightly up at Prince Fritz, whose arm she still held. "Do you have any of those in Kronenhof?"

"A great many, in our forests." The prince patted her hand. "But don't you worry, my cousins and I are mad about hunting."

Jilly's smile froze.

"You hunt dragons?" Finn asked with a straight face. "I would love to see one of your trophies!"

"Ah, no," Prince Fritz laughed. "You misunderstand! I meant that we hunt wolves, as well as boar and bear."

"Pity," Jilly said lightly. "I would love to see a dragon."

Anthea could tell that her cousin was still upset by the talk of hunting, however. For all her wild ways, Jilly had a very tender heart.

"Do you hunt, Lord Finn?" Princess Wilhelmina said, taking his arm.

"I do not," Finn said.

"It's an excellent pastime . . . for royalty," the emperor said, looking at Finn.

"It's difficult to find time for hobbies when you spend most of your days taking care of horses," Finn said. "Especially since we have had an epidemic in Coronam that killed or sickened so many of our riders."

"That was a shame," the emperor said. "We never had that sickness here."

"Of course you didn't," Anthea blurted out. Everyone looked at her, waiting for an explanation. "It's not as if it can jump over the ocean," Anthea said finally. "Disease, I mean."

"But it could be carried by people," Princess Wilhelmina said, though that didn't stop her from stroking Finn's arm.

"Yes, that's unfortunately how it spread around Coronam and Leana so quickly," Jilly said.

Oh, no, Anthea thought.

Beloved?

"Yes, it turns out that there was a very evil person who spread the disease on purpose," Jilly said.

Tell Jilly not to say her name, Anthea frantically thought at Caesar.

Then she asked Florian to pass the same plea to Caesar and then to Jilly, since talking to someone else's horse was considered bad manners. Although that was partly because most riders could only use the Way with their own familiar horses.

But while they desperately needed to find Anthea's mother, they also needed to do it with great tact and subtlety, two things that Jilly was not known for. They didn't know how close the emperor and Anthea's mother were, and how much he knew of her plans, and they needed to find out very carefully, so as not to endanger Meg and the horses.

"Oops," Jilly said, and put her free hand over her mouth. "I shouldn't have said that!" She laughed. "I'm so terrible!"

"Are you?" Prince Fritz grinned down at her. "I must know more!"

Anthea and Finn exchanged looks of apprehension, while Princess Wilhelmina got right to the point.

"Why not speak of this person?" she said. "I demand that you do!"

"Indeed," her father agreed. "Your slip of the tongue intrigues me."

"Oh, well!" Jilly put her hand to her eyes as though shy. "It's just that there's the most dreadful woman running about in Coronam!

"A disgraced Rose Maiden, you know." She tapped the rose and horseshoe pin on her jumper. "Quite horrid. She tried to kill us all—the entire country! And it's not the first time she's done something like this; no one knows how to stop her." She looked appealingly up at Fritz. "One of the reasons why I jumped at the chance to come here, Your Highness, was to get far away from that creature!"

Marius says that the Now King says that She Who Is Jilly is "laying it on too thick," Florian reported. *I find her words confusing. Is she speaking of The Woman Who Smells of Dead Roses?*

Yes, my darling, Anthea said. *Tell Marius to tell the Now King I agree. We need to rein her in.*

But the stunned silence that followed Jilly's little act was broken, not by Finn or Anthea, but by one of the guards. He had been looking at Bluebell with a very fixed gaze since taking up his position by the door and suddenly spoke to Anthea in heavily accented Coronami.

"That animal is horse? Yes?"

"Yes," Anthea said, startled at being so abruptly addressed by someone that she had forgotten was even there.

"It is spots," he said, pointing to Bluebell's gray dapples.

"Yes, she is dappled."

"But the ghosts do not spots," he said.

"I—I beg your pardon?"

The other guard was nodding now, too. "The forest ghosts," he said, as though that explained his fellow guard's comment. "No spots," he added.

Anthea looked helplessly from them to an equally confused Finn and Jilly, and then to the emperor. Her confusion became even greater when she saw that the emperor's face was turning red, chest swelling out as though he were about to start shouting. Fritz and Wilhelmina suddenly looked very young, and very much like they feared an explosion.

That explosion came, with a great, angry shout in Kronenhofer that sent the guards fleeing from the stable. The emperor was right behind them, and Anthea thought she saw him raise one hand as though to strike the men. Prince Fritz dropped Jilly's arm and fled after his father, with his sister close beside him. In seconds they were alone with their horses, but the sound of the emperor's ranting carried back to them for several minutes.

"What. Was. *That*?" Jilly wanted to know.

"I don't know exactly," Finn said, hurrying to comfort Marius, "but it would seem like there are horses here. In Kronenhof."

Anthea was suddenly struck with an idea. "If we can find these horses, I bet they could help us find our horses!"

"It looks like we have a job for your mother, Jilly," Finn said. "She speaks perfect Kronenhofer, and we need to know everything there is to know about these ghosts!"

INTO THE FOREST

"WOW, WHAT A TERRIBLE idea this was," Jilly said cheerfully.

Anthea didn't say anything. She was busy trying to push branches out of the way so that they didn't rake her off Florian's back. It was easier said than done: the forest, like everything else in Kronenhof, seemed determined to thwart her. She had already been slapped in the face more than once by an errant branch, and was wondering why no one in the Kronenhofer court had an eyebrow scar like hers.

"We're all going to die," Jilly moaned.

There was a slap and a shriek.

"I'm so sorry!" Finn spluttered. "Jilly, honestly, I didn't . . ."

"It's fine," Jilly said, sounding muffled. Anthea heard her spit. "I wanted something to eat."

"You need to be quiet!" Prince Fritz whispered loudly from behind a nearby tree. "You will scare the animals!"

"Good!" Jilly nearly shouted back.

"Shush! You shush!" came the loud whisper from another hunter.

Finn reached over and took Jilly's reins, pulling Caesar forward while she used both hands to shove branches out of the way. When they were huddled together—Finn and Marius, Jilly and Caesar, Florian and Anthea—he whispered much more softly than the hunters.

"Jilly's right, this was a terrible idea."

"Hunting with the prince is the best excuse we have for exploring the forest," Anthea pointed out, even though she privately thought that they were right. Part of her wished she were back at the palace with Lady Cassandra, who at this very moment was discreetly asking about the "ghosts."

"But we'll never find the ghosts with all these hunters," Finn said. "We're probably scaring them away!"

"Good," Jilly said, not bothering to whisper. "Let's scare *everything* away! Do you really want to kill some poor fox?"

"I'm not trying to kill a fox!" Finn reminded her. "I'm trying to find out if the forest ghosts know where Con and the others are! And we can't do that if we can't find them! Or have you forgotten?"

Jilly didn't deign to reply to that last remark.

"We are too close to the schloss, there are too many

people, and there's no mist," she said, ticking the points off on her fingers. "We aren't going to see any ghosts, who apparently only show up when it's misty, and *I* don't want to see any dead foxes."

"We are not hunting fox," said a voice at Jilly's elbow.

Jilly screamed, Finn dropped the reins to both horses, and Anthea nearly shot Prince Fritz. Fortunately, she always steadied herself and took a deep breath before she fired her gun, which Caillin MacRennie had told her was a terrible habit. But in this case, her steadying breath prevented an international incident.

Fritz laughed at her expression and horrified apology, holding up his hands in mock surrender. Anthea hastily lowered her gun, then holstered it, feeling alternately hot and cold.

"I am sorry I startled you," the prince said. "I came to say that perhaps the horses are not the best way to hunt after all.

"Will you get down and come with me?" He aimed his grin straight at Jilly.

"Why don't Finn and I take the horses back to the palace," Anthea said immediately. "Jilly, you can stay here and hunt . . . Um, what are you hunting if it's not fox?"

"Deer," the prince said. "Beautiful creatures! And delicious!"

He held up a bow; he had a quiver on his back. About half

of the young courtiers with them were thus armed; the others had long rifles.

"Deer?" Finn's eyes widened. "I certainly hope that no one glimpses the horses through the trees and thinks they're deer!" He gave the prince an angry look. "If I had known you were hunting deer . . ."

"Don't worry," the prince said. "I told my friends not to shoot your horses."

"Oh, thank you," Anthea said.

Jilly gave her a look. "Sarcasm is *my* defense mechanism," she whispered.

"We'd better go back," Finn said. "Anthea and I will take the horses. Jilly, have His Highness tell you all about archery."

Finn gathered up Caesar's dropped reins and pulled him around a little. Jilly took the hint and dismounted. She looked a little disgruntled, but after the prince held out an arm to her, she brightened. Finn and Anthea watched them walk off into the trees, chatting easily, before they turned and went in the opposite direction.

"I think it will be easier to walk than ride," Anthea said as another branch slapped her in the face.

"Agreed."

They slid off their horses and started to lead them through the forest. It was different from a Coronami forest: there wasn't a lot of underbrush to stop them, and riding seemed to put their heads level with the thickest branches. Anthea shortened the reins so that she was pulling Florian's head down over her shoulder.

I'm sorry, my love, she said. *I don't want you to get hurt.*

This is not our forest, he observed. *The trees are different. The ground. There are many creatures lurking I have not a name for.*

Nor do I, she agreed, though truthfully she hadn't seen signs of any animals besides a few small birds flitting from branch to branch.

Keeping her head down, and Florian's head down, brought Anthea's attention to the ground. It rained less here than in Leana, although the ground beneath the trees was still fairly soft and held the marks and footprints of hunters and the occasional animal. There was nothing that Anthea could identify, though.

Arthur fussed around inside her coat, and Anthea took him out and set him on the low pommel of her saddle so that he could look around.

"What do you think, Arthur?"

"Have you tried reaching him with the Way?" Finn asked. "I used to try all the time with other animals. Sheep. Dogs. The barn cats."

"Any luck?"

He shrugged. "I was convinced that an old sheepdog we used to have could understand me better than anyone else, but I never got any response back. You know, in my mind. And I had to talk out loud. But I could get him to go to other rooms, fetch things for me, like shoes and people he knew well."

"Really?" Anthea blinked in surprise. "I never thought . . ."

She hadn't tried much with Arthur. She talked to him a lot when she was alone in her room, but she had always talked to herself when she was alone. A few months ago he had followed her a great distance and come to her rescue when she had been hurt. But she couldn't tell if he had imprinted on her the way they said that baby birds did on their mothers or if he was finding her through the Way.

Should she try?

Arthur?

No.

Anthea's heart stuttered and she stopped in her tracks. Then she realized who had answered her.

Florian?

Yes, Beloved. He sounded apologetic. *I'm afraid that the Way does not work with birds. Or other beasts.*

Are you certain?

Quite.

"Florian says no," Anthea told Finn. She ran a hand down Arthur's rounded back, his tightly folded wings. "So you're not trying to talk to me?"

He turned his head and gave her a disgusted look. Finn, walking on her other side, laughed.

"Yes, Marius says the same thing. He just said that dogs

are very smart, but don't have the special bond that creates the Way."

"Ah!"

Anthea reached across Finn and stroked Marius's shoulder. She didn't want to make a fuss, but that was probably the longest thing he had said since the Incident in Upper Stonesraugh. It gladdened her heart to think that he might come all the way back to himself one day. She exchanged a look with Finn, and knew that he was thinking the same thing.

"And, no offense to Arthur, but if dogs don't have the Way, owls seem less likely," Finn said.

"You better watch yourself," Anthea said. "Arthur has been known to cough out his pellets in the shoes of people who offend him!"

She laughed and moved to stroke the owl again, but he leaped into the air and glided away. He didn't go far; the branches were too thick for that. He soon came down to land on the path before stalking off into the trees in his typically determined fashion. Anthea hurried to catch up to him, flipping the reins over Florian's neck.

"You all keep going; I need to catch an owl," she said.

She went around the base of the large beech tree that Arthur had just disappeared behind, but there was no sign of him. He was brown with cream spots, which was fairly good camouflage in Leana. But here, where the earth was darker and the leaf mold more reddish, he should have been easy to find. Yet there was no sign of him.

"Arthur? Arthur!"

"Do you want help?" Finn called from a bit ahead.

"No," she called back. "I want the horses away from the hunters. Go on, I'll find the little brat!

"Arthur! Come here!"

There was an irritated hooting noise from the left. She shuffled carefully around another tree, worried about stepping on the owl because of the thick drift of fallen leaves there. But when she saw Arthur, he was standing in a cleared space, plainly visible, scratching his claws in the dirt and watching for her.

"What are you doing?" she scolded, and leaned down to pick him up.

She froze.

The dirt that he had been scratching had a spattering of deep indentations that looked terribly familiar.

Hooves. Horses' hooves.

HOOFPRINTS

ANTHEA COLLAPSED ON HER bed with her filthy riding clothes still on, too exhausted to take them off. She had spent hours in the forest with Finn trying to find the ghosts. Unfortunately, they could not tell which direction the prints were coming from, or where they were going. It was as though a horse had dropped from the sky, wandered in a circle for a bit, and then gone back to the heavens.

But it wasn't all for naught. From the size of the prints in the mud, they were able to tell that Kronenhofer horses had smaller hooves than Leanan horses. But the prints were just as deep, indicating that these "ghosts" were fairly heavy.

"So we're looking for a small, dense horse?" Anthea had asked while in the forest, regretting the question as soon as it left her mouth. A small, dense horse? She sounded like a fool.

Finn didn't seem to think so. "Basically," he said, nodding and squinting around. "Look at the land: there's nowhere they could run a great distance; it's all forest and hills."

"They probably have to climb up and down rocky hills," Anthea mused. "I wonder if they live in caves."

"Most likely," Finn agreed.

Then Anthea noticed marks on the bark of the nearest tree, as though a large animal had rubbed itself against the trunk, scratching its side. Anthea had seen horses do it plenty of times at the farm, on fence posts as well as trees. And as with the scratch marks at the farm, there was hair caught in it.

Anthea slipped off her leather gloves and carefully plucked some of the short hairs out of the bark. They were horse hairs all right. They felt just like the winter hairs that Anthea had to constantly brush out of Florian and Bluebell and Leonidas, to keep them looking majestic and less like shaggy cows.

"They're longer," Finn said, taking a few. "But softer? And look at the color."

"Light red," Anthea said. "With some white."

"Caesar's coat is almost this color," Finn said. "But the white mixed in? No."

"So we are definitely looking for shorter, heavier horses. Longer coats, mixed colors."

But that was all they were able to discover. Anthea sighed now, staring up at the ceiling above her bed. Yes, they had a better idea of what the ghosts looked like, but that wouldn't help if they couldn't find them. Right now, their only plan for rescuing Meg and the horses relied on finding the ghosts, and they still didn't know if the strange horses would help. Anthea closed her eyes and pressed her hands into her face, sighing again.

"Don't lose hope," a voice said from her doorway. Jilly had come into the room, but it was Finn, at her heels, who had spoken.

"He's right," Jilly said, plopping down next to Anthea, who sat up. "I have a plan."

"Really?" Anthea couldn't keep the doubt out of her voice, and Jilly whacked her with a pillow.

"Simple," she said. "Divide and conquer. I stick with Fritz and his friends, who are all well connected and foolish, and find out as much as I can. If there's a princess being hidden anywhere in Kronenhof, they'll know. Meg has to be at someone's grandmother's castle or father's hunting lodge.

"You and Finn keep searching for these wild horses, and see if they can lead us to Con and the other missing horses."

"Oh, just like that?" Finn laughed. "Jilly, you've been with us! Has there been a hint of Con?"

"Well, no," Jilly said easily. "But I'm not you. Or Thea. If Florian and Thea can't find Con by the end of the week I'll eat my favorite silk scarf."

"But my mother also took one of the stones," Anthea reminded her. "There's something about them . . . they block the Way . . . If she's keeping our horses in a stable with that stone, we'll never find them!"

"There's no way they can keep Con anywhere he doesn't want to be for very long," Jilly said. "You just have to be ready for when the inevitable jailbreak comes."

FLORIAN

She Who Was Jilly was right: there was no way to contain Constantine. The herd stallion would fight his way free, to get back to the rest of his herd. To get back to his mares. That was his job.

But it was worrisome that he had not done so yet.

Of course he would not leave the mares that were with him in captivity. And Brutus, a noble and powerful stallion, if older in years. He would bring them all with him to freedom. It was his duty as herd stallion.

Even Florian, when he had carried Beloved Anthea to safety after she had been shot, had taken care that the mares with them did not fall too far behind. And he wasn't even herd stallion, not in that place and at that time.

Perhaps, though he was not fond of humans, the herd

stallion was looking for the chance to escape with the New Meg as well. Ensuring the safety of all his herd, including the mare Holly and her rider. Yes. That was right and proper for a herd stallion.

It was surely the reason why Constantine had not come to the Now King yet.

6

HUNTING

"ISN'T THERE SOME STORY about stringing yarn behind you so you don't get lost in a maze?"

Anthea looked behind her, twisting in the saddle and bracing herself with a gloved hand on Florian's broad rump. Anthea had been so confident in their plan the day before, but hours exploring the forest left her feeling dejected. Behind her there was nothing but trees. In front of her there was nothing but trees. Trees to the left. And on her right, Finn on Marius, and more trees. She gave Florian's glossy golden-brown hide a quick rub before turning back around.

"Sounds familiar," Finn agreed. "A princess? Trapped in a maze? Or . . . her lover? She spun the yarn, though. I remember that."

Anthea blushed when he said "lover," but covered it turning

her head from side to side to stretch her neck. They had been riding for hours. They decided to try a direction away from the hoofprints they found since they hadn't had any luck in that part of the forest, but without any glimpses of the ghosts at all, she felt like they were wandering aimlessly.

"Meanwhile, Jilly is taking tea with the princess and her cronies," Anthea muttered. "And I'm *cold* and *hungry!*"

Finn laughed. He reached in his saddlebag and pulled out something. He handed it over to Anthea. It was small, and round, and she almost dropped it.

"A chocolate?"

"Raspberry flavored. Your favorite," he told her.

Anthea couldn't help the smile that spread on her face. He noticed.

"I accidentally ate a violet-flavored one yesterday," he continued, and then shuddered. "Flowers and chocolate do not mix."

Anthea put the chocolate in her mouth and chewed slowly. She took a moment to check with Bluebell and Leonidas back at the palace.

Is all well?

Yes, no one has come to peek at us, Leonidas said.

I do not like when they do that, Bluebell chimed in.

I don't like it, either. Remember to tell me immediately if it happens!

Yes.

Anthea frowned, thinking how faint their voices sounded.

"How far from the schloss do you think we are, if we drew a straight line between us and it?"

Finn looked at the sky and squinted. "A mile? Two? At the most."

"I just checked with Bluebell and Leonidas, to see how they were," Anthea said. "I can barely hear them. It's like they're on the other side of a wall. Or a good ten miles away."

Finn stopped, reining in Marius, looking as if he had been struck with an idea.

"If they're less than two miles away, but you can barely speak to them, then that means that somewhere in these two miles is the standing stone!"

I do not like that stone, Florian sighed.

Anthea's frown deepened. Florian sounded so distant, too—not as distant as Leonidas, but still not as loud as he should've been when she was so close to him.

Anthea dismounted and took hold of the reins just below Florian's chin, not because she feared he would wander away, but for reassurance. Very slowly they began to creep through the trees toward the place where the Way had almost gone silent. Anthea craned her head from side to side, trying to see if there were any tall stones like the ones that had fenced Upper Stonesraugh, the Last Village of Leana, away from the world and the Way.

There was nothing. There was no strange tickle. No sudden

silence in her head. She could tell that Marius was coming closer—and she could see Finn's quizzical expression—but it felt like Marius was still miles away. It was as though she were standing right next to the stone ring, but hadn't passed through it yet.

"Oh, oh!" Anthea said aloud.

She scuffed at the leaf mold beneath her boots. There was only an inch or two of the soft dirt and dead leaves. Underneath that her boots hit hard earth. Or something else. She let go of the reins and knelt on the hard ground, scrabbling with her leather-gloved hands.

"What are you doing?" Finn said as he rode up.

"It's solid rock!" Anthea announced, sitting back on her heels. "Look at it!"

She pointed to the area she had cleared. Beneath a thin layer of dirt and leaves, the ground was rough gray rock. She took her gloves off and put a single finger on the bare rock. After a second she shuddered and pulled her hand back.

"It's the same rock," she said. "Like the standing stones in the Last Village! The whole forest is full of it!"

Dancing with Hostages

"I LOVE YOU BOTH dearly," Jilly proclaimed, briefly wrapping her arms around the two of them.

They had just told her what they discovered in the woods. Jilly released them so that she could take a glass of punch with one gloved hand and a canapé with the other, and Anthea could see her mind whirring.

"The MagTaran said those standing stones were like no other rock in the village or the surrounding hills," Jilly mused. "The Leanans who founded Upper Stonesraugh might have quarried it from somewhere near here."

Jilly looked for all the world like a smiling debutante enjoying yet another party. Her words were just soft enough that they didn't carry. Anthea did her best to mimic Jilly's easy gait and smooth brow as they moved across the floor to their customary table to the right of the imperial dais.

"And taken it all the way to Coronam?" Finn looked skeptical. "Well, I mean, it was still Leana then. But why? That's . . . thousands? Thousands of miles!"

"If they knew it could block the Way, keep it from carrying out of the village . . ." Jilly shrugged. "It would be worth it."

Now it was Anthea's turn to ask. "But why? They didn't need to hide, not back then, before the Coronami invaded."

"I don't know that they were hiding," Finn said. "But there were so many more horses back then." His voice turned wistful. "And every herd had a herd stallion. You would've had to keep them separate. The stones would have been the perfect way to do it."

"Huh, that actually makes sense," Jilly said. "I mean, if Con smelled even a *rumor* of another herd stallion, he wouldn't sleep until he had murdered them! And I'm sure he's not the only herd stallion who has ever been so . . . passionate . . . about staying in charge."

"So that all fits," Anthea said aloud. "But it does leave us with the question of how they found out about the stone to begin with."

"They probably brought their horses with them when they visited Kronenhof," Finn said. "Just like we did. And ambassadors probably had their own horses when they were living here."

"But unless they rode around in the Imperial forest, they wouldn't have known," Jilly argued. "And have you ever heard of a Leanan ambassador?"

"Well, not recently," Finn said.

The three of them chuckled at that.

"Good work," Jilly said. "But now I have to mingle."

She drained the last of her punch and went to join Prince Fritz. Anthea sipped her own punch, which was far too sweet, and watched Jilly chatting and laughing. She felt a frown creasing her own features. How would they find Con and the other horses if the entire forest was littered with the Way-blocking stones?

"Wipe that look off your face," Lady Cassandra said in a singsong whisper. "And *smile*."

Out of the corner of her eye, Anthea saw her aunt signal a waiter to clear their table. When he came over, Lady Cassandra also gave him Anthea's drink.

"Hey," she said feebly. It had been quite nasty, but it gave her something to do with her hands.

The waiter looked back, uncertain, but Lady Cassandra waved him away. Then she pointed to the gilt-and-brocade chair opposite her.

"Sit."

Anthea sat.

"I had expected far better from you, Anthea, I really had," Lady Cassandra said.

As was usual for a public place, her face was pleasant and her voice was low and warm. Anyone who wasn't listening carefully would have no idea that she was scolding her young charge.

Anthea, who had been trained in such tactics herself, felt her spine stiffen. She smoothed her expression, and adjusted the ribbons tying her fan to her left wrist as though she hadn't another care in the world. Lady Cassandra nodded in approval, but her next words were anything but approving.

"One of the reasons why I even agreed to this mission was because I thought you would welcome the chance to show off your hard-earned skills from Miss Miniver's Academy." Lady Cassandra shook her head, making the plumes in her glossy hair wave. "And look at you!"

Anthea broke protocol and looked down at herself. A lady was supposed to waft through the room as though she had no care for her appearance, no matter how long it had taken her to get ready for a social engagement. But there was also the temptation to see if something was wrong with her ensemble, because of her aunt's censure.

But Anthea's elegant ball gown was perfect: the rich midnight-blue gauze draping over a bright cerulean satin slip without even a wrinkle.

"Not your *gown*," Lady Cassandra said. And though she didn't roll her eyes, it was implied in her tone. "Of course you always look very correct . . . when you're not wearing that *man's* army coat! It's your demeanor."

"What?"

"That's exactly what I'm talking about," Lady Cassandra said.

Then she smiled and flipped open her own fan as she caught the gaze of a passing gentleman. As soon as he had moved on, she snapped her fan closed again and leaned slightly over the table.

"I expected you to charm Prince Fritz; I expected you to charm the court! To dance, go hunting, take tea with Princess Wilhelmina . . . as you have been trained to do! Think how much information we could have by now if you hadn't been busy moping around, fussing over your horses, and only dancing with Finn!"

"I—I um," Anthea stammered. "But Jilly . . ."

"That has been a pleasant surprise, I will admit," Lady Cassandra said. "But she—"

"I do beg your pardon, ladies," said a smooth voice.

Startled, Anthea looked up to see the young Kadiji man in the Kronenhofer uniform standing over her. He bowed and held out his hand.

"Forgive the interruption, but I did wonder if Lady Anthea would dance with me."

"Of course," Anthea said.

Despite her aunt's dire words, Anthea was on her feet and had her right hand correctly placed on the young man's arm before her brain could even catch up. He led her into the dance and she put her left hand up on his shoulder as he clasped her right.

"I hope your chaperone is not displeased," he said. "At

first I thought you were merely discussing the weather, or the fashions, but as I got closer it seemed much more serious."

"Only being scolded for some small slight," Anthea said with a pointed sigh. "Such is the life of a young lady!"

"Ah," he said. He looked confused. "I am not sure why a young lady as refined as yourself would need to be scolded."

Anthea smiled graciously at the compliment and dared to ask the question that had been nagging her since she had first seen her dance partner standing beside the emperor. "Please forgive my boldness, but who *are* you?"

He stopped dancing, and Anthea hurried to move them both as another couple nearly crashed into them. She had often had to lead at Miss Miniver's, since it was an all girls' school and Anthea was tall.

"You truly do not know?" he whispered.

"Er, no," Anthea said. "Should I?"

She felt a hot flush creeping up her neck. Had the emperor had a Kadiji wife? But he looked to be the same age as Wilhelmina, so how was that possible? Was he adopted? Surely that sort of information would be widely taught?

"I'm Prince Adil," he said.

"It's an honor to make your acquaintance," Anthea said automatically.

There was a long pause. Prince Adil still looked faintly shocked.

"I'm a hostage," he said at last.

Anthea stopped dancing so fast that Adil continued, and nearly dragged her off her feet. Another couple did bump into them, so they moved over to a marble pillar more out of the way. Anthea only just managed to keep herself from openly gaping at Prince Adil.

"I—what do you mean?"

"Five years ago?" Prince Adil said. "The assassination attempt on the emperor's brother, Prince Ferdinand?"

"Oh, yes, I know about that," Anthea said. "It was supposedly Kadiji spies, and by the time it was proved that the Kadiji king didn't know about it, the spies had been killed and no one knows who was behind it." She nodded firmly, having recited the facts. "Right?" she added uncertainly. The hot flush ran up her cheeks. "The Kadiji king . . . is your father, isn't he?"

He nodded. "My father and his ministers proved beyond all doubt that there had been no official Kadiji involvement. We bear no ill will to the Kronenhofer . . . or at least, we did not. And we most definitely do not want a war with them."

"But what *happened*?"

"I was walking in the public gardens after lunch, discussing philosophy with my tutor," Prince Adil said. "I was kidnapped, my tutor killed, and I was brought here. In case."

"In case of *what*?"

"In case my father lied about not wanting war with Kronenhof. As long as I am here, my father will not attack."

Anthea's hands fluttered like useless, wounded birds. One hovered around her neck, the other at the prince's shoulder.

"So you're . . . you're trapped here?" Anthea did her best not to squeak as she said the words.

Prince Adil sighed. He nodded, and then he moved them back into the figures of the dance.

"People were beginning to stare," he whispered.

"Ah," Anthea said.

Her heart was racing, and so were her thoughts. She was horrified at what she had just learned, but on the heels of her concern for Prince Adil came other, more urgent concerns.

What did this mean for Meg? Had the emperor ordered Genevia Cross to kidnap the princess so that she, too, could be held hostage? But wouldn't they have announced her presence by now? Wouldn't Meg, too, be standing on the dais beside the emperor at parties, pretending to be an honored guest?

"I have troubled you," Prince Adil said. "I am sorry!"

"No, no," Anthea protested weakly. Then she stiffened her resolve. As Lady Cassandra had pointed out: this was what she had trained for.

"I am just so terribly moved by your story," she said with the perfect amount of compassion in her voice. "I have been curious about your place at court, but I didn't want to intrude upon your privacy."

"That is so kind of you," Prince Adil said.

Anthea was certain that beneath her hand, his shoulder relaxed a little. He smiled a little more broadly. She decided to press forward.

"I hope that you are treated well?" she ventured.

"They treat me like a son," Prince Adil said. But his voice was stiff. And so were his shoulders again.

"I suppose," she said lightly, "it's a bit odd. Being treated like a son . . . who is not allowed to leave the palace?"

He relaxed again. "Yes," he said softly. "You understand."

"Poor you," Anthea said. "It must have been so strange, to be taken from one palace to another . . . and then to realize that this palace was really a prison."

Was that taking it too far? She almost held her breath as they turned around the floor in time to the stately waltz.

He nodded, however. "They did try to ease me into it. They may have even tried to negotiate with my father at first," he said. Then he sighed again.

"Oh, really?"

Anthea's heart started to thump hard again. Had there been an ultimatum? A two-week deadline? And they hadn't gone to war, yet he was still here. Was that good for Meg, or bad?

"For several weeks I was held at a manor house somewhere nearby, in the forest," Prince Adil said. "That was really the worst part. I was so cold all the time! And no one would speak to me or explain what was happening. Then I was brought here and told I would stay here as long as it took."

"As long as it took to do what?"

"I'm still waiting to find out," he said.

They shared a laugh. Not a hearty one, or a particularly joyful one, but a laugh nonetheless.

"Whose manor was it?" Anthea said, sounding only mildly curious. "I thought most of the forest belonged to the Imperial Crown."

"It does," Adil said, as though he hadn't thought much about it. She supposed he was just glad not to be there anymore.

"I wonder if it was some sort of faux rustic cottage," Anthea suggested. "Like the fake ruins in the gardens. Or a hunting lodge . . . ?"

Adil opened his mouth to answer when Finn appeared beside them.

"May I?" Finn asked, already reaching out to take Anthea's hand.

"Oh, of course," Prince Adil said, stepping aside with a little bow.

Finn took hold of Anthea and swung her away from the prince. He had to count for a moment to get into rhythm with the other dancers, but when he had, he was able to look at Anthea. And her expression almost stopped him in his tracks.

"What is it?"

"What was *that*?" she demanded, not letting her smile slip or her feet falter. "How could you interrupt me like that?"

"Well, pardon me for thinking you would be tired of flirting!" Finn said, his cheeks reddening.

"*Flirting?*" Anthea thought she might slap him. "You idiot! Adil was about to tell me where they're keeping Meg!"

CONSTANTINE

Constantine did not like feeling trapped.

He had tried his best to get himself and his herd out of this filthy box that these men dared to call a stable. He had broken doors and walls. He had trampled the men who came to bring them food, hoping to lead the others out over their bodies. But the mares had been too frightened, and then more men had come, with guns. Constantine did not fear them, but it wasn't him they aimed at, it was the mares.

Every time he tried to break free, they took one of the mares away until he "behaved." They did not beat them, but kept them in a separate room, alone, and gave them only a little water and no food. Horses did not like being alone, and for mares it was especially hard.

The mare Blossom was greatly concerned for her rider, the

New Meg. The young human filly had become dear to her and she fretted over the New Meg's well-being. She had tried to reach her rider with the Way, even as Constantine himself had attempted many times to reach the Now King. But there was no answer.

Their journey had been in the company of a large stone that kept the Way from carrying very far. Constantine found that he could not even reach out to the mares and Brutus, although the rooms they were in were only a few paces apart. The very walls were made of this strange, slick stone. He had seen it before, in a ring around the village where the Now King had found so many relics of his family's past. But it had not caused such a fog in his brain then.

There was simply too much of it here. He could not think. And if he tried to fight, to get free of the stone and the men, they would punish the mares.

Constantine stood in a corner of the filthy stable, his head hanging down. Perhaps it would be better to be dead.

8

GHOSTS

IF YOU LEAVE, PLEASE do wake me.

My love, my love, do not forsake me.

Anthea hummed the ballad that Jilly had sung during the long journey they had undertaken to Bell Hyde, the first time they had dared to go there. The journey that had resulted in Anthea being shot, meeting her mother, escaping from a moving train, getting a fever, and nearly dying. Only Florian had kept her safe and alive, delivering her directly to Finn and Jilly at Bell Hyde. In her delirium, Anthea kept repeating the words of the ballad to him.

My love, my love, do not forsake me.

I never shall, my Beloved, came Florian's reply, faintly.

Anthea, Finn, and Jilly were out exploring the forest again in a new direction, hoping to spot the ghosts and to distract

Jilly. Her cousin had practically vibrated off the sofa that morning when they took tea with Princess Wilhelmina. It had been an excellent opportunity to ask about other manor houses nearby, or who might have a hunting lodge in the forest, and Cassandra and Anthea had carefully discussed how to ask this casually, in case Wilhelmina knew where Meg was, or if she found their interest suspicious and told her father.

Jilly, of course, had been all for them simply asking point-blank if the princess knew that her father had kidnapped another princess. Anthea had been shocked when Lady Cassandra had musingly said that if anyone could get away with something like that, it was Jilly. But in the end they had decided on subtlety, and while Jilly had sat and fidgeted with her teacup and spoon, Anthea and Cassandra had made idle conversation.

And learned precisely nothing.

Finn had tried his luck with Fritz, who was too busy looking at a dog racing form to pay attention. And Adil couldn't be found at all. The morning had been deeply frustrating, and Anthea was sure she wasn't the only one saying a silent prayer to find the elusive ghosts soon.

The three of them zigzagged for hours, barely talking, mindlessly looking out into the trees. So when Florian stopped suddenly, Anthea pitched forward over his neck.

Beloved! What is it?

Florian pawed at the rock and whinnied.

Look!

Anthea turned her head and looked in the direction Florian's long nose was pointed. She immediately grabbed hold of his bridle for reassurance.

"Oh," she said.

Finn rose slowly to his feet. Jilly gave a barely audible chuckle.

"These are some very pretty ghosts," Jilly whispered.

They all stood and stared in silence at the line of wild horses watching them.

Anthea held her breath, too scared that any movement might cause the ghosts to disappear just as quickly as they came. Although they were partially hidden by shadows and foliage, she could tell that Finn had been right about their build; they were shorter than the Leanan horses, but stocky, with thicker bodies and muscular legs that could barely be glimpsed through the swirls of mist. Their manes stood up along their necks, thick and coarse and perhaps only a hand-length long, unlike the long fall of mane on the Leanan horses. They were beautiful, but so very strange.

Anthea looked between Jilly and Finn. They hadn't discussed what they should do if they actually *found* the ghosts of the forest. Jilly nudged Finn, who looked confused.

"You're the king," Jilly whispered. Anthea nodded agreement.

"But I think they're *mares*," Finn protested.

Their whispers clearly carried to the horses, who shifted

their hooves and flattened their ears. There were three of them: a reddish mare speckled with white whose coat Anthea recognized from the hairs she had found caught on the rough tree bark, a cream-colored beauty with a black-tipped mane, and the smallest, an indeterminate brown, who was edging away already.

Shall I? Florian inquired.

Yes! Anthea thought with relief. *Should you ... introduce yourself? As herd stallion in this place?*

I can try, he agreed.

"Florian will talk to them," Anthea whispered.

The ghosts twitched at the sound of her voice. The chocolate-colored mare disappeared back into the mist, and Jilly clapped a hand to her own mouth to keep from calling out to her. Florian took a very tiny step forward and raised his head.

Greetings, gentle mares, he said.

Anthea was thankful that the Way wasn't a language of words so much as images, odors, and feelings. Florian's Kronenhofer was probably even worse than her own!

I am the herd stallion of—

He didn't need to finish that sentence. By "stallion" the mares were gone. By the time Anthea and her companions had slowly and unthreateningly edged over to where they had stood, the mist had thickened, the ghosts had long faded away into their familiar forest, and all that was left were more hoofprints and a single cream-and-black tail hair.

9

A Fast Set

EVEN AFTER THE ONSET of evening forced them to return to the palace, Anthea couldn't stop thinking about the wild horses. And she wasn't alone in this: the next day, she and Finn and Jilly spoke of nothing else. If they hadn't also been tasked with finding Meg and their missing horses, the discovery of horses on foreign soil would have consumed the imagination of every rider and every Leanan horse.

But unfortunately they had to "play nicely" with their royal hosts, which meant accepting Fritz's invitation to lounge about in his sitting room this afternoon, instead of getting back out to try and speak to the horses.

"Don't tell me, Lady Thea, that you don't know how to do the trot! You'll break my heart!"

Anthea opened her mouth to say that she wasn't a lady.

That she didn't like strangers calling her Thea. That she did, indeed, know how to do the "trot," thank you very much, both on a horse and on the dance floor.

But what came out was a little shriek as Prince Fritz grabbed her hands and began yanking her around the drawing room carpet. Anthea tried to make eye contact with Jilly, but her cousin was deep in conversation with one of Fritz's friends, hopefully digging for information about the mysterious hunting lodge, as subtly as she knew how.

The music was far too slow for a trot. But Miss Miniver had taught her girls what to do if they were unfortunately paired up with an inept partner. Anthea began to gently lead the prince around the floor with small movements of her shoulders and hips so that he was none the wiser about losing control.

"You see," he crowed when they stopped bumping into furniture and were indeed doing a fast trot around the room. "I can teach anyone to dance!"

Once the song ended, Fritz rejoined his friends by the gramophone and Anthea gratefully took a seat on the sofa between Finn and Princess Wilhelmina, who did not look at all pleased.

The princess had never bothered to hide her disdain for Anthea and Jilly, and their sudden interest in her father's properties didn't help. Anthea had no idea what the princess must think about all their seemingly innocent questions, but it clearly wasn't flattering. When the Horse Maidens had entered the room she had looked at them as if she'd just smelled something nasty. But Anthea hadn't failed to notice that Wilhelmina seemed willing to talk to Finn, and so she got right to the point before the princess clammed up again.

"Have you ever seen the ghosts in the forest?" Anthea said, giving the princess her most winning smile.

"Do I look like someone who wanders around the forest at night?" Princess Wilhelmina snapped.

"So you don't hunt, like your brother?" Finn said politely, leaning ever so slightly against Anthea so that she had to sit back against the sofa.

"No," Princess Wilhelmina said.

"I'm afraid it's not really something that interested me, either," Finn said. "Although it was very generous of him to take us along. I much prefer a fast ride on a horse on an open road, with the sun on my face and wind blowing past. I like to see how fast I can go, and how far."

Anthea was about to ask him what he was talking about when he put that subtle pressure on her shoulder again. She sat back, and the princess leaned across her like she wasn't even there.

"Ah! The open road! Such a thrill!" Princess Wilhelmina said with such delight that she suddenly looked less like a statue. "I have never driven a horse, of course, but I am very fond of motorcars. Do you drive motorcars?"

"I confess that I have only driven a few times, and the vehicle that I drove hardly deserves to be called a motorcar!" Finn laughed with self-deprecation.

Anthea couldn't help but smile, thinking of the Thing. It was a homemade motorcar that Uncle Andrew and Caillin MacRennie had put together for the farm from other old parts, at least one of which had been a tractor.

"I learned to drive in a Bundt-Schmidt Peregrine," Anthea offered. "And my uncle Daniel has a Bundt-Schmidt Eagle. They come from Kronenhof, I believe?" She asked the question innocuously, as though she didn't know the answer already.

Now Princess Wilhelmina gave her a look that didn't make Anthea feel as though she had a dirty face. She gave her a gracious smile and a nod.

"The Bundt-Schmidt Eagle line is very fine," she said. "Very luxurious seats, a big engine. My father has two. I have been toying with the new Bremeni cars, myself. Smaller, faster. The engines are quite loud, but it can't be helped. I have a Pritienne, and an Armentie."

Anthea had heard of those, but she had never seen either of them in real life. She was able to make suitably impressed noises and get an "Amazing!" out of Finn without having to step on his foot. She would have to tell Lady Cassandra later that some of the lessons she had given Finn were sinking in.

"Would you like to try riding a horse?" Anthea asked. "It's

different from driving a car, but having done both, I find riding horses more thrilling."

Princess Wilhelmina frowned. "How fast can a horse go? As fast as a motorcar?"

Anthea went to answer and then sat back again. It occurred to Anthea that any of the horses could easily outstrip the Thing, but that they had never tested them against a real car. She glanced at Finn.

His eyes were gleaming. "We've never raced a horse against a motorcar," he said, leaning toward the princess again. "Which of your cars is faster?"

"The Pritienne," Wilhelmina said without hesitation. "We should do this immediately; it looks like rain tonight. We don't want the road to be wet." Her eyes sparkled and her face was flushed, her movements animated.

"Definitely not," Finn said, getting to his feet and reaching a hand across Anthea to help the princess up. "If you could have someone clear the drive? And mark the finish? Let's say a quarter of a mile for the first course."

"Perfect," Wilhelmina said. "I shall give the order and have my Priti brought around while I change.

"Which of your horses will you be riding? Which do you think is the fastest?"

Finn froze, as did Anthea. Across the room, Jilly looked up from her conversation.

"Oh, Florian is definitely the fastest," Jilly said. "What are you all talking about?" Her eyes gleamed much like Finn's had. "Are we racing?"

"Do you, too, like racing?"

Wilhelmina looked at Jilly in the same avid way she was looking at Finn: the boring, potentially threatening, guests had turned out to be worth her while after all.

"Florian is the fastest, but Juniper and I have been practicing," Jilly said. "Trying to get used to each other."

"Oh?"

Anthea had noticed, of course, but hadn't much thought about it. Before she had gotten permission to ride Caesar, Jilly had mostly ridden a mare called Buttercup, who sadly had been one of the horses abducted.

"Caesar has excellent staying power," Jilly said. "But Juniper is simply *shocking* at sprints!"

"So," Wilhelmina said. "Three to one? Hardly fair." But she had a catlike smile on her face. "I accept the challenge!"

She swept out of the room. Her brother and his cronies followed, already placing bets, most of them unaware of what they were even betting on. The three riders looked at each other.

"What have you done?" Anthea said, feeling the anger rise through her like a tide. "The princess doesn't want to race *me*! Or Jilly! She wants to race *you*. You're the one flirting with her!"

"I'm not flirting . . ." He trailed off, looking away from Anthea.

"I'm sorry, are we really going to have this fight right now?" Jilly demanded as she grabbed both of them by the arm and began to drag them out of the room. "We have to change and get the horses ready!"

"Florian is the fastest horse," Anthea said. "But there's no way he could win against a racing car!" What if they lost? Would the princess shun them in disgust?

"I know, I know," Finn said. "But Wilhelmina was finally talking to us! I thought this could lead in to asking her about—"

He stopped as both Anthea and Jilly shushed him.

"About the stones or the lodge or Meg or anything," Finn whispered.

"Wilhelmina is her father's favorite. Lady Cassandra has been telling us that we have to get close to her. We finally have a way to do it!"

Finn was right, and Anthea's mind was already moving ahead to the next problem.

"Marius isn't up for this," she said, and Finn nodded agreement. "And you have to make a good showing, to impress the princess and earn her confidence. We *need* to know about the hunting lodge. That's our best bet for where Meg is being held. Even if Wilhelmina doesn't know, she would still be a huge asset."

"I *know*," Finn mumbled. "Do you think Leonidas will let me ride him? He's quite fast."

"He would. But Florian is the fastest." Anthea paused, steadying her breath. "I'll ride Bluebell. That way it will be girls against boys. Against motorcars."

"Thea, are you sure?" Finn asked, a crease forming between his blue eyes.

"No," Anthea said. "So I'm not going to talk about it." She managed to avoid slamming the door in his face when she went in to change.

RUNNING THE RACE

BELOVED, I DO NOT like this, Florian said.

I know, my love, I know, but you are good and brave, Anthea told him.

She stroked Bluebell's neck, more forcefully than was necessary. The storm cloud gray mare snorted and pawed at the paved drive.

I don't like this either, the mare said. *But no one asked me. No one ever asks me!*

I'm so sorry. Would you rather that I rode Leonidas? Anthea tried to make it sound like an innocent question, knowing the proud mare would hate the idea.

Perhaps, Bluebell replied maddeningly.

Anthea ignored her, since she was more concerned about Florian—brave and strong and wonderful Florian. It was hard to believe it had only been a year since Anthea returned to the Last Farm and reunited with her beloved horse.

And now here they were, in a foreign country, standing next to a strange motorcar, being watched by strange people, and Anthea was telling her darling, her beloved, that he must let Finn ride him. She remembered how wild Florian had been before she had ridden him, how dangerous.

I would never let the Now King fall, Florian assured her.

I know, my darling, I know!

But secretly, where he couldn't hear her, she kept on worrying. What if the car's engine backfired and spooked him? What if the princess veered into Florian or Bluebell? How good of a driver was she? And she surely wouldn't hurt one of the horses on purpose?

Would she?

There were too many things that could go wrong.

Finn's expression told her that he was all too aware of it. He was sitting on Florian's back like a burr, tight and close and curved. Anthea had never seen him look less confident. He normally sat as Andrew taught them: straight and still and relaxed.

Jilly moved Juniper up close to him. She was smiling, at ease. "You better not lose, or else you'll embarrass all of Leana," she taunted. Finn straightened his back and shook his elbows a little to loosen his arms.

She is too bold! Bluebell said in shock.

But it did work, Anthea said.

"Even though it was rather rude," she finished aloud.

At that moment, Princess Wilhelmina stood up in her car and waved gaily at them. The car was beautiful. Low and narrow and shaped like a bullet, it was painted a smooth cream color. It didn't have a roof, and seated only two, so the scarlet leather interior was on full display. It looked fast and expensive.

The princess wore a cream-colored driving coat and had wound a white silk scarf around her hair to keep it out of her face. Servants had made a thick chalk line on the long drive to mark the start. It was clear that the princess challenging someone to a race was nothing new.

What was new was that it was three horses she was competing against. News of the race had spread, and many members of the court were gathered on the front steps of the palace. Servants who couldn't find an excuse to stand outside peeped from behind the curtains.

Wilhelmina had moved her motorcar to the far right edge of the drive, the gleaming grill just behind the chalk starting line. Anthea walked Bluebell over to where Jilly was talking to some of Fritz's friends, including Prince Adil.

"Allow me to hold your coat, Lady Anthea," Prince Adil said.

She almost pulled the coat closer around herself in protest, but then she saw Jilly's raised eyebrow. Putting aside her heavy wool coat did make sense, and she trusted Adil to take care of it more than anyone else here.

"Thank you, Your Highness," she said.

"I have placed my wager on you," he said.

Anthea felt herself blush.

"I have money on Jills," Prince Fritz said. "Her horse is a stunning beast!"

Jilly and Juniper both glowed. Juniper was indeed beautiful: like Caesar she had a golden mane and tail, but where his body was reddish, Juniper was a rich dark brown.

"And that is your herd stallion?" Prince Adil asked, pointing to Florian and Finn, who had taken up the position next to the motorcar.

Anthea looked at Florian with great affection and concern. In the weak sunlight that broke through the ever-present Kronenhofer clouds, his golden-brown hide gleamed. His mane and tail were black, neatly trimmed and freshly brushed by Finn, who had done his best to quickly bond with Florian by giving him a quick going-over.

Finn caught her gaze. "Florian will take good care of both of us," he said. "It'll be fine!"

Jilly stroked Juniper's neck, her halo of curls practically crackling with energy and her face alight.

And now Fritz was standing on the side of the drive, nearest to Jilly, and he was holding up a white handkerchief. Anthea gripped the reins, holding herself ready. She could feel every one of Bluebell's muscles bunched and waiting beneath her. She could feel Florian and Juniper on either side of her also waiting, and hear the caged roar of the motorcar.

"Ready?" Prince Fritz cried.

"Yes!" Jilly answered.

Wilhelmina revved her engine.

Anthea and Finn just looked at each other. Then she quickly looked back at the prince.

He dropped the handkerchief.

Anthea dug her heels into Bluebell's sides, but the mare had already leaped forward. Loosening the reins so that Bluebell could stretch her head and neck forward, Anthea crouched low on the mare's back. Now was the time for clinging like a burr, and Anthea wished she had taken the time to shorten her stirrups, as well as braid Bluebell's mane, which immediately began to whip her face.

On her right, Finn was also lying low along Florian's neck again, and they quickly pulled ahead of Bluebell. To Anthea's surprise, Princess Wilhelmina and her motorcar were still level with Bluebell. Anthea checked her left, and saw that Jilly and Juniper had taken the lead.

Through the veiling of Bluebell's mane, Anthea watched with awe as Juniper streaked forward. Her gait was smooth, the reach of her legs so long, that Jilly hardly moved from where she crouched on her mare's back.

Florian had pulled level with her, but his more muscular

frame made him look like he was working harder. His hooves pounded the drive, and Finn was rocking with the movement.

The motorcar shifted gears. Anthea heard it, and she felt a tremble run through Bluebell. Anthea crouched as low as she could, murmuring words of encouragement that were whipped away by the wind.

Bluebell's early burst of speed had taxed her, and they could both sense the motorcar shooting ahead of them. But no horse could keep up with it. Sending soothing thoughts through the Way, Anthea let Bluebell settle into a comfortable pace. Finn was putting on a good showing with Florian, and Juniper was a revelation, so it was all right with Anthea if she and Bluebell brought up the rear.

And because they were behind, they saw exactly what happened.

And because Anthea knew motorcars, she knew that it wasn't Princess Wilhelmina's fault, and that she had done everything possible to avoid an accident.

And because Bluebell's eyes were on Florian, the mare knew that it wasn't Finn's fault, and that he did everything possible to prevent Florian from being hurt.

The whole thing happened in a matter of seconds.

Anthea was off Bluebell's back before Finn hit the ground. She was kneeling at Florian's side before she even stopped screaming.

11

A NOTE

ANTHEA SAT WITH HER back against the makeshift stable wall, Florian's head in her lap, and stroked his mane. Early morning light was starting to filter through the window, but Anthea hadn't slept at all. Her legs were stiff and her back ached, but she wouldn't move.

When Anthea and Florian had been hurt on their first, horrible adventure, Florian had stayed outside in the garden at Bell Hyde so that he could look at her window, but she had been too weak to visit him. Dr. Hewett from the Last Farm had told her later that she had had a terrible shock, and that her brain wasn't working correctly while it healed, but she blamed herself nonetheless. Her darling, her love, her Florian had been alone with his injuries!

She wouldn't leave him again.

"You must forgive Finn," Lady Cassandra ordered. "This can't go on!"

Anthea stared at her, uncomprehending, for a full minute. Lady Cassandra looked like some sort of holy vision, standing in the muddy shed-turned-stable, wearing a beautifully tailored navy blue suit over a cream lace blouse, her upswept hair crowned by a dashing navy straw hat crowned with lavender silk roses.

Meanwhile, Anthea had straw in her hair and down the back of her blouse, which was dirty and missing a button. She had taken off her boots to get more comfortable, and now her socks were so unspeakably filthy she didn't want to put her boots back on.

"I'm not angry at Finn," Anthea said at last. She was so tired she felt stupid, like every thought was wading through treacle on its way to her mouth. "Did he . . . say that?"

Anthea looked around the stable. Finn had been with her all night, but he wasn't there now. She blinked and scrubbed her face with both hands.

"I assumed you were hiding here because you were angry," Lady Cassandra said, sounding bemused. "Heaven knows I would be angry if someone played with one of my dogs and then hurt the poor dear!"

Anthea felt terrible. Stiff and dirty and tired and hungry and worried.

Beloved?

In an instant she was kneeling beside Florian again.

What is it, my darling?

Florian lay in an extra thick layer of clean straw on the floor of his stall. There were bandages around both forelegs, and the left front foreleg was splinted as well. There were smaller sticking plasters on the multiple cuts on his left side that he had gotten when he fell, hard, on the rough drive.

You should go, eat, sleep, he said.

I will not leave you!

But I am not alone now, he said. *You are right here, and you will be back, I know. And the others are here, and the Now King and She Who Is Jilly are nearby.*

I can have someone bring me food, Anthea said.

Servants had brought food earlier, she remembered vaguely, when Jilly and Finn had been there. Juniper was bruised, scraped, and more than a little shaken, and Jilly had been caring for her while Finn helped Anthea. But Anthea had dozed for a while and hadn't seen Jilly and Finn leave.

"You have to go inside, wash, eat, and be ready to accept the princess's apology," Lady Cassandra said briskly. "As well as Finn's."

"Finn doesn't need to apologize," Anthea said, hazily. "It wasn't his fault."

She would have had no problem accepting the apology of the princess, though, but none was forthcoming. After all: the race was Wilhelmina's idea, even if the accident wasn't her fault.

Having pieced everything back together, after they had gotten the horses safely back to the stable, it seemed that one of the sleek racing car's tires had popped, and the explosion had made her swerve, nearly hitting Florian. In order to avoid being hit, Finn had steered Florian, who was running flat out, into Juniper. Both horses had gone down in a tangle of legs, screaming and thrashing, and Anthea's heart had nearly stopped when she saw Florian's leg twist. It turned out to be only a sprain, and even more miraculous: Jilly and Finn had thrown themselves clear and received nothing more severe than some bruises.

"I'm fine," Anthea said. "I just want to sit with Florian for another day."

But Anthea, Jilly, and Finn were planning on going out to the forest that night to try and talk to the wild horses.

Beloved, you cannot go into the forest without me! Florian sounded more agonized about this than he did about his injuries. *You must wait for me to be well again!*

I will not let harm come to Our Anthea, Leonidas said. He never dared to call Anthea "Beloved," that was Florian's name for her alone, but this was as warmly as he had ever said her name, accompanying it with images that spoke of home.

Finn can ride Marius, and Jilly can ride Caesar, Anthea said. As much as she didn't want to leave him, they couldn't wait to find Meg and the horses.

We will let you know if Florian needs anything, Bluebell said.

It will be easier for him to rest without worrying about stepping on your feet.

"I take it by your vapid expression that the horses are trying to convince you of something?" Lady Cassandra said crisply. "They seem like sensible creatures; I am sure they are telling you to come with me now." She opened the door of the stall.

Anthea allowed herself to be led out of the stable by her aunt. Lady Cassandra fussed and picked straw out of Anthea's hair all the way to the palace doors. A cold wind whipped down, making her shudder, and Anthea put her hands in the pockets of her coat.

Something crackled in the left pocket—a piece of paper. She pulled it out, a half sheet of paper folded in half again, with her name scribbled on it. Her brain was starting to work now, and she thrust it back in her pocket before Lady Cassandra noticed.

When they entered her room, Finn leaped up from the chair where he had been sitting and peeling an orange. His face went so pale it was practically gray. "I am so, so sorry, Anthea," he said, his voice low.

"It wasn't your fault," Anthea said sincerely. "He'll be just fine."

"But it *is* my fault," Finn said. "I'm the king! I should never have put any of our horses in danger! Racing them against a motorcar . . . The best outcome was that they would be exhausted, not to mention humiliated! What if one of them had spooked and run into the car? What if someone had come down the road in the other direction and run into them head-on?" His shoulders slumped, his head bowed. "What if Florian had *died*? The herd stallion for this place . . . and your beloved," he finished in a low voice that was barely audible.

Anthea felt something hot stirring in her chest. Finn cared, not just about horses, but about her? Of course he did . . . he had kissed her once! On the cheek, and given her a necklace . . . but still . . .

"You did what you had to do," Lady Cassandra said. "As a king. To win over the princess."

"But it was a mistake," Finn said. "It wasn't worth it!"

"Oh, it absolutely was," Jilly said, coming back from the bath. "Not only did I have three people who never spoke to me before boast about where they had seen wild horses—well, they said ghosts, same thing—but I won fifteen crowns off Fritz and thirty from Heinz!"

"Jillian! Gambling?" Lady Cassandra was shocked.

"*Winning*," Jilly said. "I want to buy some scarlet silk and have a gown made like Wilhelmina's last night, but you know . . . lower here." She gestured at her chest.

"Jillian!"

Anthea started laughing. It wasn't that funny, but she couldn't stop. She clutched at Finn's hands to hold herself up as her laughter almost made her fall over her dirty socks. Finn started laughing, but he was blushing, too. He gripped her hands tighter, propping her up as she gave in to her sobs.

She tilted forward until her forehead was on his shoulder, and then Finn let go of one of her hands so that he could put an arm around her and rub her back.

"All right, that's enough of that," Lady Cassandra said, dragging Anthea away and propelling her toward the bathroom. "You need a bath."

"Finn," Anthea heard Jilly say as she was being pushed down on the edge of the nearly full tub. "We have to do this right now, while we have the sympathy from the accident. Tell Wilhelmina that you're not half as worried about Florian as you are about your dear cousin Meg."

She started to say more, but Lady Cassandra closed the door with a snap. She surveyed Anthea with her hands on her hips.

"You are simply a mess," Lady Cassandra said.

"Er, thank you?" Anthea said, wiping her face with a filthy hand.

Lady Cassandra clucked her tongue, but she was thoughtful as she helped Anthea peel off her muck-encrusted stockings and dirty clothes. She tossed everything in a corner of the room, and gently eased Anthea into the bath. Anthea was surprised at how stiff and sore she was despite not taking a fall herself. But she supposed sleeping in a nest of straw wasn't ideal.

"I have to confess," Lady Cassandra said suddenly. "When I was given this assignment I assumed that it would be you and me against Jillian. Trying to make a young lady of her. Getting her to comb her hair or wear a gown . . . but she isn't like that."

"No," Anthea said, scrubbing her face with a rough cloth to hide her astonishment. "She's not."

"That place was so barbaric," Lady Cassandra said. "And the horses were so frightening!" She sounded very young, very much not like herself. "Andrew was so kind, but . . . I just couldn't do it!"

Anthea had dropped the soap and the washcloth, but she didn't notice. In all the time they had been together, Lady Cassandra had not once talked about the Last Farm or Uncle Andrew or her marriage in any way. Her demeanor didn't invite questions, and Jilly had never wanted to talk about her mother, even when she wasn't right next door.

"Why did you go?" Anthea dared to ask. "To the farm, I mean? How did you meet Uncle Andrew?"

"The late Queen Juliane sent me. Mere weeks after I took the Rose. I was to travel the coast, painting." Her eyes had a faraway look. "I am a gifted watercolor artist, you know! And while I was there, I was supposed to find out how the exiles felt about the Crown.

"One day a storm came in, one of those sudden storms along the coast. It would have ruined all my work, but a young man was passing and helped me find shelter.

"While we waited out the storm we talked, and then he offered to take me to his house to warm up and have some supper." She sighed. "Andrew was so handsome," she mused. "We were married so quickly, I didn't dare to tell the queen, or anyone! And after all, they could never know anything about Andrew and his family. He swore me to secrecy that first day.

"It was all so strange and exotic and romantic at first. But I never liked the horses. Horrible beasts!"

She shuddered. "One day, a sweet young man—a boy really—was trampled by his horse. The creature simply turned on him, for no reason. Every bone in his body must have been broken; *if* he lived, he surely never walked again! But as they were taking him away to the hospital, all he could do was rave about how it wasn't the horse's fault, and to tell his horse he would soon be back!

"That's when I knew I had to leave. It was absolute madness, and I wanted no part of it!"

The bath was growing cold, but Anthea didn't dare move to turn on the hot tap. She didn't want anything to stop her aunt from telling the rest of the story.

"Jillian was born a few weeks later. I thought of taking her with me, claiming she was a foundling I had adopted. But once Andrew found out that I intended to leave, to pretend none of it had ever happened . . . well, he begged to keep her, saying it would be easier to convince everyone that I had spent the previous year painting and questioning exiles, without a baby in tow.

"So I left them both. I tried to visit, but I could never bring myself to go farther north than Blackham. I tried to get Jillian to come south, once she was old enough to know her own mind, but . . . well, you know she would never leave."

"But how did Josephine know?" Anthea asked.

"When Queen Juliane died, Queen Josephine inherited her Rose Maidens, as was tradition. She interviewed each one of us extensively to find out what we had done at court. And that Josephine is a canny one! She wouldn't let up until I told her the whole story, without the horses. I told her I had eloped with an exile, and regretted it, and she was tactful enough not to press me about what crime he had committed. She offered to send me back to Leana, but I told her I had seen poor Anthony savaged by a wild beast, and never wanted to return there."

"Anthony?"

"Anthony Hewett was the young man's name," Lady Cassandra said. "I've never forgotten it." Her face crumpled as she plucked at her skirt, still distressed by the memory.

"But the queen wrote to me immediately after meeting Jillian, and told me every detail." Lady Cassandra closed her eyes briefly. "She even sent me a photograph of all of you with your horses. I recognized Jillian at once. She has my dimples, and Andrew's eyes." Lady Cassandra blinked rapidly, coming out of her reverie. "The queen was good enough not to be angry that I kept the horses secret."

She smoothed her skirt and turned on the hot water tap, correctly guessing at the coldness of the bath. "I had better make sure that Jillian and Finn get the information we need," she said, one hand on the doorknob.

"Aunt Cassandra?" Anthea said.

"Yes?" Her voice sounded muffled.

"I thought you should know. Anthony Hewett? He didn't die. He can't ride; it hurts his back. But he can walk. He went to medical college, and now he's the farm's surgeon. Dr. Hewett helped develop the vaccine that cured the Dag."

"*Doctor* Hewett?" Cassandra whispered, blinking. And she went out.

12

Nine Days, Then Eight

"I FEEL LIKE WE should be calling them," Jilly whispered. "I don't want to scare them."

"Calling them how, though?" Anthea said. "Here, horse, horse?"

"I don't know, it just seems rude to sneak up on them!"

"They can feel us coming," Finn said.

"Can they?" Anthea asked.

She kicked at the rocks underfoot. Not all of them were the slick gray rock that blocked the Way, but enough of them. She had Leonidas, but she was walking him, one hand tight on the reins just below his chin. Finn had gone a bit ahead of them with Marius, and on Anthea's left Jilly was walking Caesar.

"Here, horse, horse, horse!" Jilly shouted, causing Caesar to skitter sideways. "There's no beardy emperor with us! You can come out!"

"Jilly!" Finn said severely.

Anthea made a shushing noise at the same time, looking nervously over her shoulder in the direction of the schloss. Jilly tossed her head and walked on.

Anthea could tell that her cousin was upset. She was kicking the rocks and fallen leaves, and Caesar's ears had gone flat. Anthea hurried to catch up to her.

"Did it ever occur to you, and my mother, and Finn, that I might actually make a good Rose Maiden?" Jilly suddenly burst out.

Anthea gaped at her. She spluttered when she could finally speak.

"What? I mean ... I didn't think you wanted ... you always ... you never wanted to be one!" When she recovered she added, "You made fun of me for my manners when I first arrived!"

"Well, your nose was stuck in the air!" Jilly said. "You deserved to be teased!

"I still don't *want* to be a Rose Maiden," she continued. "*But*, I could be a very good one! No one gives me any credit for the times I don't ride off barefoot on Caesar, but instead sit around drinking repulsive hot weed water and talking about clothes with Fritz!"

"Hot weed water?"

"Do *you* like chamomile tea?"

"Not really."

"Well, Fritz loves it! He owns a tea farm somewhere in the

south. If I have to sample one more cup of special weed water that tastes exactly like every other cup of weed water, I shall scream!

"But I won't scream," she went on. "Do you know why?"

"Why?" Anthea asked, caught between laughter and amazement.

"Because I'm not a *child*," Jilly said heavily. "Because I'm not an idiot, either. I may be outrageous at times, and I know that I'm a disappointment, but I'm not *that* much of a disappointment, thank you very much!"

Anthea stopped, pulling Leonidas up short.

"Jilly! You're not . . . you don't really . . ."

Anthea was shocked to find her throat closing up, her eyes prickling.

"You've never been a disappointment to me," she choked out, fierce.

"Lady Cassandra, on the other hand," Jilly said with a voice that would have sounded glib to someone who didn't know her.

"No," Anthea said. "Jilly, you have to talk to her. She didn't . . . she's not what you think."

Anthea wondered how much Jilly knew about her parents' history. She didn't think it was her place to divulge all of what Cassandra told her. "Lady Cassan—your *mother* used to be so scared of horses," Anthea said, "but I think if you talked to her, you'd find that—"

"Giiiiiirls," Finn drawled.

"Don't you 'girls' me," Jilly began, then stopped with a sharp gasp.

Anthea had looked up and froze. They were in the same place they had been before: the rise of land and scattered boulders on the edge of the forest. And there, in the moonlight, were two of the wild horses, watching them.

Silently, Anthea and Jilly moved forward so that they stood close to Finn and Marius. Their horses, too, were silent, despite having been coached beforehand to reach out in a friendly manner to the ghosts. Anthea loosened her white-knuckled grip on Leonidas's bridle, stretching and flexing her cramped fingers.

Ask them their names, she urged him.

They are mares, he said, and Anthea was taken aback by how scandalized he was by her suggestion. *I could never presume!*

Is that why we're all just standing here? Anthea demanded, hardly needing Leonidas to nod in affirmation.

My Own Jilly says we must do something, Caesar said to Leonidas, who passed it on to Anthea. Presumably it also went to Finn via Marius, because Finn silently nodded.

Marius says they are very frightened, Leonidas reported.

Marius was standing a little in front of the rest of them.

Anthea thought the ghosts looked defensive, ready to attack, the way they were arranged on higher ground, their ears back and their bodies still as the rocks around them.

"Hellooo, ladies," Jilly said in a soft singsong, taking a small step forward. "We only want to talk."

The ears of the wild horses went back even tighter to their skulls. One of them pawed the ground, and another took a step forward, lips slightly curled to show strong, square teeth.

"Stop," Finn hissed. "Only the horses should speak to them," he added in the faintest of whispers, his lips barely moving. "Who should be herd stallion in this place? Leonidas? Caesar?"

Anthea felt a stab of humiliation on Marius's behalf. Or . . . was she feeling what Marius was feeling? Leonidas had taken an anxious sidestep just then, and Finn had reeled back, letting go of Marius's reins. The poor horse's feeling of rejection had been that strong.

Marius stepped forward, walking straight toward the strange horses. Finn made a half-hearted grab at him, but Marius kept going.

Anthea was glad: she didn't want the wild horses to think that they were keeping Marius against his will. Nor did she want to spook them. The wild mares were grave, watching Marius carefully, but unmoving as he approached. He didn't get too close, but stopped right at the foot of the broken rise of boulders they were standing on.

What are they saying? Anthea asked Leonidas.

He is telling them about us. That we come from far away. That you and the others know our language.

You mean the Way?

That is what you call it, yes.

Marius should ask them if they've seen Constantine, Anthea said. *Can you ask him?*

Marius is very bold to introduce himself to new mares, with no herd stallion, Leonidas said stiffly. *We must wait until it is the right time.*

"Ask them why no one from the schloss has come after them before," Jilly whispered urgently. "We're a stone's throw from the grounds! How do they not know about the horses?"

"They know. People have seen them," Anthea whispered, not taking her eyes off the mares.

They were backing up, startled at the rising tones of Jilly's voice. Anthea had seen skittish horses, sad horses, sick horses . . . she had never seen horses so close to bolting, however. They were more like birds that wanted to peck at the crumbs of a picnic, but were ready to fly away to the top of the highest tree if someone chewed too loudly.

Oh, he asked them, Leonidas said. *Oh no.*

The mares tossed their manes, they whickered in unease, and then they turned to leave. Marius went after them, ears pricked and neck extended as though he wanted to catch at their tails and stop them.

Anthea got impressions from Marius, but not actual words. It was how the horses spoke to each other: there were sounds and scents, images and flashes of color. Marius was trying to tell them it was safe, that they should stay with Finn and Anthea and Jilly. He told them that they would be cared for, fed, sheltered.

"We want to help you!" Finn cried out in Coronami and then in accented Kronenhofer. At the same time, he sent thoughts at them, loudly enough for Anthea to "hear" that he was saying the same thing through the Way.

Marius, trying to help, bugled and went from a fast walk to a trot as the mares scattered. They leaped like goats through the fall of boulders and up the small rise. This time when Finn put out a hand to stop him, gently laying it on his haunch, the stallion stopped.

The mares were gone. Marius, almost sadly, lifted his head and called out again. Finn moved forward to take hold of his bridle, whispering something to Marius and stroking his forelock.

What is that? Leonidas asked.

"What is wh—" Anthea began, but stopped short.

A horse had answered Marius's neigh, crying out in full voice and clearly not one of the mares. It came from too far away, and there was a raw, angry quality to it. A familiar tone.

"Finn!" Anthea whispered, as though he couldn't hear it, too.

He turned to her, his eyes wide and bright in the moonlight. "Con," he breathed out. "It's Constantine!"

CONSTANTINE

These people, this whispering Woman of Dead Roses, this Bearded King, they would not leave him be! And now there was greater distress to be found. He himself was feeling weak and sick, but the mares, and even Brutus, were gravely ill.

It was not the water. It was not the food. Constantine would not let his people be poisoned! But they stood all day in this close darkness. There was no clean air to breathe. There was no wind to blow the foulness and stink away. There was no sunlight to warm their coats.

Constantine knew that he was failing his people, that he must get them out of that place, but how? What little strength he had he saved for lashing out against the Bearded King, who came to him each day, reaching out foolish, sweating hands to attempt to touch him. Constantine had bitten him, had tried to kick and trample him. The bite, alas, was the only blow that connected. Constantine regretted, too, that he had not bitten the man's hand clean off. How dare he touch the herd stallion? How dare he touch Constantine, on whose back the Now King alone might ride?

Constantine knew that She of the Dead Roses could kill him at any time. She said it to him often. He couldn't let that happen, as it would leave the mares and Brutus without protection. Brutus, noble beast, would take up the care of the mares and try to see them to safety, but he was near on forty years old, more than twice Constantine's age, and not of the royal bloodline, either.

No, Constantine had to get out of this place. He had his duty to his herd, back home. That was the only reason why he had feigned a greater illness than he felt. The reason why he had staggered, and refused what meager food he was given.

And so at last, when they had taken him outside at night, to see if the fresh air would strengthen him, he had been able to see the walls around this place, see their tall gray stones that kept him from speaking to the others.

But the gray stone did not keep out the sound that came, of a horse calling out. Nor did Constantine fail to recognize the voice of one of his own herd, a young foal he himself had sired.

Marius. Marius was nearby!

Constantine answered.

13

UNEXPECTED GUESTS

"I'M GOING TO RENAME Con," Jilly grumbled. "I'm going to call him The Ghost from now on!"

"They can't be far," was all Anthea said. "I mean, we all heard him!"

Leonidas stumbled on, though Anthea knew he was very tired. It was probably closer to dawn than any of them wanted to contemplate. They had been zigzagging slowly through the woods, moving out from the point where they had heard Constantine, away from the boulder where they had seen the wild horses.

"Can't be far?" Jilly said, sitting back in frustration and making Caesar halt. "I have no inkling of where we even are, but there's nothing out here but more trees and rocks! We've gone farther than we've ever been from the palace, but there's no hunting lodge, there's only . . . *trees*!"

Why does She Who Is Jilly hate trees so much? Leonidas asked.

Ignore her, darling, she's just being dramatic, Anthea said with a sigh. *But do you know the way back to the palace?*

I . . . I am sure I could find it, he said, his voice uncertain. *We are very far from it. I think.*

"Then we should be close to wherever Constantine is!" Anthea spoke aloud in frustration.

But like Jilly, she was reluctant to go any farther. She wondered if Finn was having any luck with looking for the ghosts. He had gone in the opposite direction, hopeful of tracking the wild horses, since Marius seemed to have such a rapport with them. But the rocks made it so impossible to pass messages through the Way. He could have found a magical underground kingdom ruled over by stout red-maned mares for all they knew.

"Let's go back," Jilly said. "We can't do anything out here in the dark! If Con was nearby, they must have moved him!"

Anthea opened her mouth to reply and yawned, making her jaw pop painfully. Slumping in the saddle, she wondered how long it would take for them to get back. Before she went to bed, she still needed to check on Florian, too.

It took them over an hour to wend their way through the trees to the palace grounds. Finn was right at the edge of the great lawn, leading Marius and looking dejected. He didn't even need to ask if they had found Constantine and the others, but Anthea shook her head at him anyway. They were all empty-handed, exhausted, and filthy.

The only good news was that Florian was resting comfortably when they got into the stable. Anthea fed and groomed Leonidas and staggered bedward, one arm thrown around Jilly to keep them both on their feet as the sun crept over the top of the trees.

When they got to their rooms in the palace, they found Lady Cassandra waiting. She had drawn a hot bath in both girls' suites, and she was standing by Anthea's bed holding out a pink gown.

"Breakfast with the emperor," Lady Cassandra said tersely. She herself wore a lovely lace morning gown with a wide lavender satin sash. "Hurry."

She shut the door with a bang. Anthea blinked stupidly at the closed door and then hurried to take off her clothes and hop into the bath. She was sure that her hair smelled of horse, but there was no time to wash it. And she knew it would just get horsey again in a few hours, when she took Bluebell for a ride. But she did brush it as vigorously as she could.

She had her gown half-fastened and her hair was in a great cloud of static when Jilly ran into the room. She was wearing her favorite Tenduhai-style silk ensemble, with a long tunic and wide trousers in a vibrant shade of green with embroidered flowers.

"Your mother is going to murder you," Anthea said, eyes wide.

It was the sort of thing that they were all used to Jilly wearing back at Last Farm. At home. Not here. Not with the emperor.

"You are not going believe me," Jilly said as she began to do up the rest of the roughly nine thousand tiny pearl buttons that ran up the back of Anthea's gown. "But this was *her* idea! I had started to put on that blue linen gown that looks like one of your sailor suits, and she stopped me!"

"The blue gown? You weren't going to wear that," Anthea said with a snort.

"I was too!" Jilly tugged Anthea's hair with unnecessary force before gathering it with a ribbon. "I thought it would impress everyone with how demure I could be. But my mo— Lady Cassandra actually said that she would rather that I *made a splash*. And that now is not the time to hide our true colors!"

Before Anthea could ask more questions, Lady Cassandra swept into the room.

"What are you talking about?" Lady Cassandra's voice was uncharacteristically shrill. One of her dogs whined anxiously. "We have to go down to breakfast right now."

"We're hurrying," Jilly grumbled.

"Before we go I need to tell you something," Lady Cassandra announced. "I read the note in your coat pocket, Anthea."

Both girls gasped, Jilly in outrage, Anthea because she

couldn't believe she had forgotten about it. Lady Cassandra looked unapologetic as she hurried on.

"There was no signature, and it was printed very plainly to disguise the handwriting. Quite clever," she said. "It looked like instructions or directions of some kind. It said, 'Back to the oak, turn to the Star only a little, but mostly east.' Does that mean anything to you?"

Anthea frowned. "Perhaps." She felt like she should know, like an itch in her brain. But she was so tired she was more worried that if she walked too close to her bed, it would suck her in and she would sleep for days.

"Well, think about it," Lady Cassandra said. Then her expression changed, and she looked tense again. "But not during breakfast. I do suspect something," she admitted. "Never forget, girls, that we are in enemy territory, and the days until war begins are fast disappearing."

On that cheerful note, she herded them out the door, her dogs following.

"If we're hurtling toward war, shouldn't we be armed?" Jilly argued.

"You're as armed as you will ever be, Jilly," her mother said. "If you're not ready to fight now . . ." She shrugged.

Before Anthea could raise her eyebrows significantly at Lady Cassandra's use of Jilly's nickname—the first time she had ever done so in Anthea's hearing—they arrived at the room where they were to breakfast with the royal family.

"No need to announce us, we are expected," Lady Cassandra said to the footman.

He hurried to throw open the double doors, because her ladyship did not break pace. She simply aimed herself at the breakfast room, like a ship at full sail, bringing Anthea and Jilly and the dogs along in her wake. It was a move that Miss Miniver would have greatly envied, and it reminded Anthea to stand tall and take tiny, measured steps, not striding as she did crossing a paddock.

Lady Cassandra reached the empty chair at the foot of the long table, which she rested her hands on lightly to survey the room and those present.

Anthea fetched up at her aunt's left, Jilly on the right. The room was intensely golden, lit by a chandelier as well as the bright sunshine coming in from the floor-length windows on the far wall. For a moment, all they could do was stand and blink and let their eyes adjust.

"Ah, there you are, Anthea," said a woman's voice. A rich, cultured, *familiar* voice. "His Imperial Majesty was so kind to wait for breakfast for you. We mustn't keep him waiting any longer while you gape at the décor."

Jilly let out a small scream.

Beloved? Florian's voice was like a shout in her head. *Beloved? What is it? What is wrong? Is it The Woman Who Smells of Dead Roses?*

No, but it's almost as bad, Anthea replied, shaking her head to make sure she was really seeing what she thought she was seeing.

Almost as bad?

Uncle Daniel. Aunt Deirdre. The ones I lived with before I found you, my love. Her eyes adjusted to the light, and she saw who was sitting beside her elegant aunt. *And even my cousin . . . Belinda Rose!*

Anthea was so taken aback that she had to hasten to school her features, but feared it was too late. Everyone else was there, she saw belatedly: the emperor, Princess Wilhelmina, the princes Fritz and Adil. And her aunt, uncle, and cousin, all the way from Travertine.

"Oh, my word!" Jilly was clutching the edge of the table like it was a lifeboat. "I'm so sorry! For a minute I thought it was Genevia Cross sitting there!"

"Jillian," her mother said in a low warning voice.

Anthea didn't see the resemblance, other than the upswept dark hair. But then it occurred to her that Jilly had only seen Genevia once, and that was under very stressful circumstances. And Jilly's antics did give Anthea a chance to recover.

"Oh, Uncle Daniel! Aunt Deirdre! What a surprise! We had no idea you would be joining us!" Anthea said as graciously as she could manage. "You will have to forgive us for being late; it was entirely my fault. You see, one of my horses took a fall yesterday. I was seeing to him and did not receive this pleasant invitation until just a moment ago!"

She smiled at the emperor. "Apologies, Your Imperial Highness! And I'm so honored to be asked to dine with you and your family . . . and mine!" She gave a bubbling little laugh and moved around the table to kiss Aunt Deirdre, and then Uncle Daniel, on the cheek. "Dear cousin!" She petted Belinda Rose's head, which she knew would drive the younger girl wild.

In the year since Anthea had last seen her, Belinda Rose had grown quite a bit, and now wore her golden hair held back at her nape with a ribbon the same way that Anthea did. She was also wearing a morning dress suited to a much more mature young lady, and pearl drops dangled from pierced ears.

Anthea wondered if she was still a tattletale who liked to bribe others to do her mathematics homework.

"You will have to forgive Jilly's reaction to seeing you," Anthea went on smoothly, exchanging bows and curtsies with the princes and princess as she moved around to an empty seat beside Prince Adil. "She has heard so much about my mother, Genevia Cross, but seen her only once; my mother was rampaging across a small, plague-stricken village with a party of mercenaries, resulting in the destruction of a historic manor house, and the kidnapping of a number of important persons."

Several people in the room gasped. Anthea wasn't sure which ones, but it hardly mattered. She had said what she had said. They were too close to their deadline to mince words, and now Daniel was here? Without fanfare, without warning? What did that mean? Was he working for the Crown, trying to make peace? Was he simply on holiday and had called at the palace to visit the emperor?

When Anthea had lived with Daniel and Deirdre, they were always talking about their highly connected friends in Kronenhof, because Uncle Daniel had previously been the Coronami ambassador there. Anthea couldn't remember specifically if they had mentioned Emperor Wilhelm, but it wouldn't surprise her.

Or were they working for her mother?

"Yes, I am so sorry," Jilly said, sliding into a seat next to Fritz. Belinda Rose was on his other side. "The light was in my eyes, and I had a moment of panic when it reminded me of that awful, awful day!" She shook out her napkin with a snap and laid it across her lap.

"What are you *wearing*?" Belinda Rose asked Jilly.

"Belinda Rose," Aunt Deirdre said in a quiet singsong, tapping the back of her daughter's hand.

"I suppose you've never traveled to Tendu," Jilly said archly, as though she had. "But you must know how rich their silks are!" She stroked the sleeve of her tunic, and Belinda Rose blushed, looking envious.

"I thought this would be a pleasant surprise for you, Lady Anthea," Emperor Wilhelm said, waving to the footmen to begin serving the hot dishes. "Your uncle and his charming

wife and daughter arrived quite late last night. We had not
expected them for another week, so it was a surprise for us as
well. But always a welcome one." He said this last as though it
were just the opposite.

"Next week?" Lady Cassandra turned wide eyes to Deirdre. "Why, Dee Dee! I didn't know you were coming to Kronenhofer! In your last letter you only mentioned going to the
seaside to continue recuperating!"

Anthea froze in the act of taking a poached egg from
the proffered tray.

"Are you . . . have you been . . . the others . . . ," she
squeaked.

Anthea had completely forgotten about the Dag ravaging
Coronam and Leana in all the worry and drama of traveling to
another country to find Meg and Constantine and the others.

"Have you been well?" Anthea managed.

"Well, we all had a fever," Aunt Deirdre said, waving a
long white hand as though it were of no consequence. "It was
not the Dag, thank goodness, but one can't be too careful, and
with little Daniel Charles still so young, we decided to move
to the seaside until it was safe."

"Oh, that's right," Lady Cassandra said, sparing Anthea
the awkwardness of having to admit that she hadn't known
that her new cousin's name was Daniel Charles, or indeed that
her uncle had his long-awaited heir. "Daniel Charles! What a
charming name!"

"Yes, he's such a dear little man!" Aunt Deirdre smiled.

"It must be so bittersweet for you to hear about other people's babies, having had none of your own."

Anthea's jaw dropped at the dig, and she noticed Princess Wilhelmina's did as well. She had been following the conversation with a keenness that Anthea suspected her father had demanded.

Jilly sucked in a huge, audible breath. Emperor Wilhelm and Uncle Daniel had been talking quietly at their end of the table, but now stopped and looked around as they sensed the sudden tension in the room.

"My mother was so invaluable to the Crown that she had to put aside her family in order to continue serving as a Rose Maiden," Jilly announced. "It has been difficult for my father and myself, but we know Mother's devotion to the queen comes first."

"Thank you, Jilly," Aunt Cassandra said. Her voice was serene, but Anthea saw her hand shake as she put it on top of her daughter's.

Aunt Deirdre and Belinda Rose gaped. Anthea could see that they had had no idea that Cassandra and Jilly were related until now. But she saw Deirdre's eyes widen as she took in the similarity in their features and the familiar way they were sitting together.

Princess Wilhelmina seemed to thaw even more than she had at the idea of a race the day before. She leaned toward Jilly, offering her a plate of sugary pastries.

"I, too, grew up without a mother," she said. "It isn't easy.

But how wonderful that you can be together now." Her voice held a husky note of sadness. Her mother had died years ago, and she would never again be able to sit with her at breakfast.

"Thank you so much," Jilly said sincerely, taking a pastry and offering one to her mother as well. "And thank you, of course, for all your concern about Juniper and Florian."

"How are they today?"

"They are—"

"You brought them *here*?" Uncle Daniel's voice was higher than normal with well-bred shock. "There are *horses* here on the grounds?"

Aunt Deirdre half rose from her seat, one hand clutching at Belinda Rose's shoulder. Belinda Rose's mouth was a perfect O, and her face had gone white.

"You're saying that this very palace is host to those . . . those beasts? With their parasites and diseases?" He looked at Emperor Wilhelm in outrage, and the emperor swelled and rose to his feet, ready to fire back. "Do you not know about the devastation they brought about in Coronam?" Uncle Daniel went on, heedless.

Everyone was standing now. Anthea wasn't even aware that she had risen to her feet, still clutching her napkin.

"My goodness! Daniel, we should leave at once!" Aunt Deirdre gave Wilhelmina a sickly smile. "Your Highness is probably unaware of this, but horses carry terrible diseases! We got out of Travertine just in the nick of time before the horse pox nearly destroyed the city! We were so lucky that we were warned, and even then we thought it was too late!"

"Warned?" Anthea asked. "Who warned you?"

She had written to her aunt and uncle, out of a sense of duty, but not until after the epidemic had begun. She hadn't warned them of anything. Had it been the king? The queen? Or merely her aunt's garden club gossip?

"The *Dag* wasn't caused by horses," Jilly said at nearly the same time.

"We have it on very good authority otherwise," Uncle Daniel said. He looked directly at Anthea for the first time. "I had hoped that your being here meant that you had put aside your vulgar fascination with the beasts. But instead you brought them here to plague His Imperial Majesty?"

"She said one of her horses was hurt when she came in," Prince Adil remarked to no one in particular. "But perhaps some people were not listening."

Fritz openly guffawed at this.

"Who told you the horses caused the Dag?" Anthea demanded. Her heart was racing, and she had a strange feeling that she knew the answer.

"Girls, tone," Lady Cassandra chided both Anthea and Jilly. "I think everyone needs to sit down and talk civilly!"

"Now, Daniel," she went on reasonably, "you know very well that the horses don't carry disease, or King Gareth wouldn't keep them at his Bell Hyde residence, where his wife and daughters are all learning to ride! And Deirdre—you really must tell me where you got that divine gown! But also . . . *who* warned you that the Dag was coming?"

No one sat down. No one seemed to know what to say. Fritz looked like he might be ready to applaud. Wilhelmina looked more than a little concerned, although Anthea wasn't sure whether it was just pure embarrassment. All of Anthea's training made her want to sit down, shake out her napkin, and pretend that these outbursts had never happened.

But she didn't. She stood strong and stared down her uncle.

"It was—" Belinda Rose began, but her mother's hand flashed up and over her mouth and back down in an instant.

Aunt Deirdre was very pale, and Anthea thought that her aunt was silently cursing herself for being so foolish. Prince Adil, whose remark had been largely ignored, cleared his throat, and when everyone looked at him, he was looking only at Anthea. He rolled his eyes toward her uncle, and then widened them. Having no idea what he meant by that, however, Anthea returned her attention to Uncle Daniel.

"You see, Anthea," he said, and then Anthea stopped listening.

Beloved?

Florian? My darling? What is it? Are you well?

Beloved! You have to—

What? I have to what?

Anthea unwittingly took several steps toward the door. Jilly was moving away from the table, too, her face screwed up in concentration. Anthea turned her head to give her excuses to the emperor, but froze when she caught sight of him and Uncle Daniel.

They were looking at each other, and Daniel was murmuring something. The emperor flicked a finger at Anthea, and then nodded. Anthea backed away from the table unconsciously and noticed Adil trying to get her attention.

"The letter," he mouthed at her, and patted the breast pocket of his jacket, raising his eyebrows.

Anthea just barely kept her jaw from dropping. Adil had sent the letter! It must be instructions on how to find the manor in the forest. She felt like a fool for not realizing and tipped her chin in the barest nod to show that she understood.

She collected herself, resolving to use the note immediately after breakfast to try and find the manor, when she felt a sudden violent surge of emotion from the horses. All of them. She could almost hear their screams with her ears, the feeling was so loud.

She and Jilly were halfway to the doors when they were thrown open. The footmen were standing there, looking as stunned as Anthea felt. One of them pointed down at the ground. Arthur was striding purposefully toward her across the scarlet carpet.

As soon as she said his name, however, he turned and

launched himself into the air, flying low through the corridors toward one of the arched doors that led to the gardens. Anthea and Jilly raced after him, calling out to the horses, but not getting any answer. When they reached the lawn that stretched down to the stable, there was the sound of splintering wood. Heart in her throat, Anthea stopped short as the door of the stable burst open and Marius surged through. Jilly shouted the stallion's name, but he didn't answer, didn't stop, just disappeared into the forest.

14

MORE MISSING HORSES

BELOVED?

Florian!

She could hear him much more clearly now, but his voice still wasn't as strong as it would have been at home on the Farm. *Florian?*

"What just happened?" Jilly huffed as they ran. "Where did Marius go?"

"No clue," Anthea said.

Arthur, still flying ahead of them, veered to the left rather than through the shattered door of the stable, so the girls followed.

"Arthur! Where are we . . . Florian, no!"

Florian, bandaged and with straw sticking out of his mane and tail, galloped out of the stable. He came straight toward them, and Arthur, as though it were planned, swooped around and landed on his back. Bluebell and Juniper were just beyond him, looking into the forest at the edge of the palace grounds, and Caesar had followed Florian out of the stable and was heading for Jilly.

"This is why I'm wearing trousers," Jilly said, as though it had been her idea.

Anthea rolled her eyes. Florian bent his front legs for Anthea to hop on, but she hesitated.

Are you sure you should be doing this?

I am well, Beloved, Florian assured her.

She grabbed a handful of his long black mane and pulled herself up so she was sitting sideways on his broad back. Arthur climbed up his mane to get out of her way, and let himself fall into her lap when she was mounted. Jilly leaped onto Caesar with much more ease, and they wheeled around to go across the garden to where the mares were gathered.

Where is Leonidas? Anthea asked as Florian broke into a trot and then a canter. A more urgent thought struck her. *Where is Finn—the Now King! Did something happen to him? Is that where Marius has gone?*

The Now King has asked Leonidas if he could ride him, and Leonidas has said that you would not mind. They only went a little way into the forest, to find the wild mares.

Where did Marius go, then?

I do not know where Marius has gone, Florian said in a

worried tone. *Perhaps he is jealous of Leonidas, or wants to find Constantine on his own?*

Oh no! Why?

Anthea knew that Florian didn't have the answer to that, and he knew that she didn't really want one. So they just continued on, picking their way around the decorative flowerbeds and statuary to the edge of the forest. Most of the palace gardens had a tall wall around them, but not here, since Prince Fritz came and went often with his cronies, hunting and riding and picnicking.

Leonidas and the Now King went that way, Bluebell said, pointing with her nose. *We will show you.*

Anthea wanted to say no, to tell the mares to go back to the safety of the stable. But she knew that they would hate that. Nor was the stable as safe as it could be, with the emperor popping in and out without permission, and now with Uncle Daniel here.

As though reading her thoughts, Jilly spoke.

"I think it's your mother," Jilly announced as they picked their way carefully into the forest, letting the mares go first to lead them toward where they had last seen Leonidas and Finn. "I know I panicked when I saw your aunt . . . but I still think there's something going on there. I know you say that they don't have any contact . . . but how can we be sure? Who else but your mother would know to tell someone to leave Travertine just before the outbreak of the Dag?"

"Your mother is here?" Finn called out to them from behind a tree. He came trotting around one of the large trees astride Leonidas.

"No, she's not here," Anthea said. She paused. "Well, I mean, she's probably here somewhere. Just not at the schloss.

"No, it's Uncle Daniel and Aunt Deirdre and Belinda Rose, which is its own type of hell, to be honest."

Dear Anthea, I told the Now King that you would not mind if he rode me, Leonidas said, pulling Finn forward so that the stallion could nuzzle the hem of Anthea's skirt.

Of course I don't mind! Anthea assured him. She reached over and grabbed one of his ears, giving it a gentle tug.

"But what happened?" Jilly asked, impatient. "What did you do to Marius?"

"Me?" Finn was deeply offended. "Nothing! I swear! I thought I would take Leonidas out and just wander a bit, see if we could find more hoofprints, and he suddenly said Marius was leaving! We heard Marius crashing past, and you yelling, and he came toward you." Finn pointed to Anthea, and Leonidas hung his head.

"Well, of course he did," she said, tugging his ear again.

"Oh yes, it's only natural," Finn said. "But we need to find Marius now."

Anthea noticed that Finn didn't have a saddle on Leonidas, either. They were all riding bareback, unarmed, and not sure where they were going. She adjusted Arthur in the well of her lap. His claws would probably shred her skirt, but she didn't want to risk him being swept off her shoulder by a low branch.

"So, do we think Marius went to find Constantine? Or those mares?" Anthea asked as they kept going, slowly, their eyes on the ground for any sign of a hoofprint.

"Does it matter?" Jilly let out a bitter laugh. "We don't know where any of them are!"

"We'll just follow his prints," Finn said. Then he cursed under his breath.

Leonidas sidled, not liking this outburst from a strange rider. Anthea put a hand up and adjusted her ruffled collar to keep from reaching out to Leonidas and making Finn feel worse. She knew exactly what he was thinking, because the horses—at least Florian and Bluebell—had been thinking it, too.

Finn had given up Marius in favor of Constantine. Neglected him, even. And then, when Constantine was kidnapped and Finn needed him, Marius had given him his all and nearly died. And now he was in a strange land with his adored rider, trying to help find the herd stallion, stuck in a garden shed while Finn rode Leonidas, and pretending that as soon as they found Constantine Finn wouldn't ignore Marius in favor of Con again.

Anthea nervously adjusted her ruffles and pleats. She had a nagging feeling that she was missing something, forgetting something beyond trying to forget poor Marius's desperation, and wondering if he wasn't better off going wild in the forest.

Arthur had come to get her.

She had been standing at the table.

She'd dropped her napkin, staring at Uncle Daniel.

No, Aunt Deirdre, who was next to Belinda Rose, who was sitting between her mother and Prince Adil.

Adil.

Adil patting his breast pocket, widening his eyes, mouthing something at her, reminding her of the note he had sent.

"The note!" Anthea shrieked.

"What?" Jilly shrieked in reply.

Leonidas did sidle then, and Caesar as well. Florian just kept going. His ears were keenly forward despite Arthur sitting between them, and he didn't seem to notice that Anthea had nearly lost her seat on his back.

"When I was coming back from the stable, after that stupid race and that stupid crash," Anthea babbled. "In my coat! There was a note from someone!"

"And?" Jilly demanded.

"It was directions, the kind you read about for buried treasure," Anthea said. "I didn't know who it was from, or what it meant. But Prince Adil was signaling to me just now . . . he must have put the letter in my pocket when we were racing—he held my coat!" She clapped a hand to her forehead. "The hunting lodge! He's telling us where it is!"

"Do you have the note?" Finn asked eagerly.

Anthea shook her head. "But I remember it, it was so odd! 'Back to the oak, turn to the Star only a little, but mostly east,'" Anthea said.

"What? Is that supposed to mean something?" Jilly demanded.

"We're going the right direction," Finn said. "I think."

"How can you tell?" Anthea asked.

"Well, if the oak is the one at the edge of the forest, right where the lawn ends and the trees begin, then we go northeast from there," Finn explained.

"What?" Jilly said again. "What about the other oaks?"

"And which star?" Anthea said. She frowned. "Oh, wait: it's 'star' with a capital, do you think . . . ?"

Finn nodded. "It's the Guide Star that sailors use to tell north. The note wouldn't be any good if we couldn't decipher it at all. So I figure it has to be the most obvious answer.

"And there's only one oak in the gardens," he said to Jilly.

"But there's . . . there's giant trees . . . ," she said, her nose wrinkled.

"Beech, mostly," he said.

"How do people know these things?" Jilly said. "They're just . . . trees!" She blew her curls out of her eyes in frustration.

"Because it's useful," Finn answered.

"I suppose. So, north and east it is," Jilly said, adding more conversationally, "So Adil is helpful as well as handsome?"

Finn's head jerked around at this, but Anthea ignored them both. Her back hurt from riding sidesaddle without a saddle, which meant that she had to sit both very upright and twisted, and she wished that she'd had time to put some trousers on. Searching the woods for missing horses and people was hard enough without having to do it in a fragile muslin gown.

I would never let you fall! Florian said, indignant.

I know, darling, I know!

I carried you even when you were sick, and—

I know! You— What is that?

Florian slowed and stopped, so smoothly that Anthea was in no danger of falling. But he could hardly keep going when in front of them, just through the thickly entwined trees, the ground was torn into great ruts and ditches.

"Oh, hello," Jilly said, reining in Caesar beside Florian. "Methinks these tracks ring a small bell in my brain!"

"We found the schutzer-whatsit," Anthea breathed.

"And it passed through here not long ago," Finn said, pointing.

It was true: the churned-up mud and underbrush still looked fresh, but not too fresh. They would surely have heard the machine if it had passed by recently.

"I hate to tell you both this," Jilly announced after they had all stared at the deep tracks for a minute, "but I'm lost. Utterly. I have no idea where we are, and I think we've gone a lot farther than we have before."

"I don't know that we've gone in this direction before," Anthea agreed.

"Also," Jilly said with a hint of hysteria in her voice. "I'm lost on a philosophical level. Should I be looking for Marius? Meg? Con? The wild horses? Thea's awful mother? What are we even doing in this country?"

"All of them," Finn said grimly. "We're going to find all of them. And then we're going to win."

"Win what?"

"Win the war we didn't start," Finn said. "By bringing everyone home."

"Except Genevia?"

Jilly was calming down a little, so Anthea didn't see the need to answer. Especially since she didn't know the answers.

Clinging to Florian's back, Anthea let him pick his way carefully over the outer ridge of half-dried mud and step into the deep, regular tracks left by the schutzer. The forest seemed endless, and she questioned how much they had actually explored over the past few days. They had always been able to ride back to the palace in a matter of minutes, an hour at the most. Even the majority of the prince's hunting expeditions took place in what was still, technically, the palace grounds.

We have never gone in this direction, Florian said, and Leonidas concurred. *We have mostly gone south and east of the palace.*

All three horses were going slowly and carefully up the

thick, churned tracks. The way the massive treads cut into the earth made it easy to see that it had come from the south, but farther east, and made a sort of curve north that they were following now. What would they do when they found it, though?

When we find it, we will find the New Meg, Florian said.

I hope you're right.

I am.

Is this the way that Marius went?

I don't think so.

"Um, just so you know, Florian is not going the way Marius went," Anthea said.

"What?" Finn reined in Leonidas. "Why not?" He was craning his head to look around.

"Florian says that soon we will find the New—I mean . . . Meg."

"Is he sure?" Finn looked around as though expecting to see the Coronami princess pop out from behind a tree.

"Well, we've looked south," Jilly said practically. "And found nothing except rocks! Also, my motto is: Where there's a schutzer, there's your mother!"

"That's your motto, is it?" Anthea asked in amusement.

"I'm going to embroider it on a cushion," Jilly said serenely. "As soon as we find Meg and go home. And I learn to embroider."

"So, speaking of embroidering," Anthea said.

"Must we?" Finn said, but Anthea ignored him.

"I just wanted to ask about what happened just now? In the breakfast room?" She looked over at Jilly, who continued to stare straight ahead at Caesar's ears as though nothing was more fascinating. "With Aunt Deirdre and your mother?"

"Wait, what just happened in the breakfast room?" Finn said.

"Honestly, Thea, I don't know how you put up with those people for as long as you did," Jilly said, sounding breezy but still not taking her eyes off Caesar's ears. "Your uncle, staring over everyone's head like his mind might be soiled by laying eyes on a mere mortal. Little Bettina Rose—"

"Belinda Rose."

"Little Bathilda Rose looking like she's been sucking on lemons. And then your aunt, Thea! Your aunt!" Jilly didn't move, but Caesar gave a little hop forward as though he had been prodded.

"Aunt Deirdre is, um," Anthea said when Finn raised his eyebrows for an explanation. "Well, she—"

"She thinks she's the queen," Jilly said. "She's actually how I imagined Josephine would be, before I met her."

"Yes, that's it exactly," Anthea said, feeling a rush of relief that someone else understood. "It's very . . ."

"Just breakfast was exhausting," Jilly said. "I can't believe you lived with her for three years!"

"Anyway, Finn, you didn't miss much," she went on. "We

barely had a chance to eat, that Deirdre woman was horribly insulting, and then Arthur came to fetch us."

"How *did* Arthur know to come and fetch us?" Anthea said, reaching to ruffle the bird's feathers.

I told him that we needed you, Florian said. *And he went.*

You said he didn't speak your language! Anthea said accusingly.

He doesn't, Florian said. Then added, after a moment's reflection, *But he isn't stupid. A trained dog could have fetched you as well.*

"Are you as smart as a trained dog?" Anthea asked Arthur.

In answer he suddenly flew up into the air and ahead of them. Anthea was about to call after him, but then she felt the ground quake and grabbed Florian's mane tighter. She adjusted her seat on his back just a little and leaned forward to try and squint through the trees ahead.

"Did you feel that?" Jilly whispered, and Anthea and Finn nodded.

Up ahead, the wide trail of destruction they were following took a sharp curve into the trees. Finn moved forward on Leonidas and signaled for them to follow as he went across the schutzer's track and up into the trees on the opposite side of it. They picked their way through the ruts and back onto smoother ground, though with the tree roots and underbrush it was only marginally better.

But now Anthea was sure she could see something different

through the trees. Something neither tree nor shrub nor even a hill of upturned dirt. It was smooth and regular and gray.

"A wall," Finn whispered.

"It's not that awful stone," Jilly said. "Well, not all of it."

The wall was made of various kinds of local stone, most of which was gray, but some of which was indeed the slick, Way-blocking kind. Clearly whoever had made this wall had no idea what that stone did, and had merely been looking for rocks the right size and shape. The path of the schutzer curved up and ended at a large wooden gate.

There was a lot of rock and debris around the base of the wall by the gate, and Finn pointed to it. Silently he mouthed the words, "That's new." Taking a second look, Anthea saw that he was right. The wood of the gate was new and unvarnished, and the rocks showed fractures. It seemed likely they had made the break in the wall by simply driving the schutzer through it.

"I'm gonna look," Jilly whispered.

She rode Caesar right up to the wall, a few paces from the gate. Alarmed, Anthea and Florian moved right up along-side it as well, and Finn and Leonidas went to Jilly's other side.

"Hold steady, Caesar dear," Jilly said.

She put her hands on Caesar's withers and got herself into a kneeling position on his back, then from there she braced her hands on the wall and stood. Anthea could see how carefully still Caesar was standing, but even so she let go of Florian's mane in case she needed to catch her cousin.

"I'm still too short," Jilly said in disgust.

"Then get down," Finn whispered.

"No, just let me try this first," Jilly said.

She reached as high up the wall as she could and felt for a toehold with one of her kid slipper–clad feet. Anthea was on her knees and then standing on Florian's back before she knew what she was doing. She grabbed Jilly's shoulder to stop her cousin from trying to scale the wall.

"Just let me look," she hissed, and Jilly subsided.

Anthea was several inches taller than Jilly, and Florian was a good hand's-width taller than Caesar. Anthea could easily grab the top of the wall, and by stretching onto her toes, she could just see over it into the garden beyond.

"What do you see?" Finn asked, starting to kneel on Leonidas's back. He was wearing heavy boots, though, and couldn't stand without hurting Leonidas.

"Well," Anthea said, her voice coming out very high. "I've found the standing stone they stole from the Last Village, and—" She let out a gasp. "And Meg!"

FLORIAN

Florian hurt.

His bones ached; he had scratches and scrapes all over his body. His sprained ankle throbbed and so did the hip he had landed on when he had fallen in the road. One of the mare Juniper's flailing hooves had caught him just behind his left ear, and there was a lump there that he could still feel when his heart beat too hard.

Picking his way carefully along the rutted track had been more painful, and wearying, than he wanted to let on. Holding his back still so that Beloved Anthea could stay on even though she had no saddle and was sitting sideways, which was very awkward and made his hip hurt worse.

But none of that mattered. They had found the New Meg! They had found the place where that strange stone had been taken. Florian hadn't minded being in the Last Village, with its ring of stones. He could speak plainly with Constantine and Brutus, and with Beloved Anthea, of course. The ring around the village seemed meant to keep intruders out, or separate herd stallions so that they would not be jealous.

Having nearly every rock and pebble and wall made of the stuff was horrible. Florian hated this place more deeply than he had ever hated anything in his life. It was as though The Woman Who Smelled of Dead Roses had created this forest just to torment him and his companions. He was the herd stallion, until they found Constantine, and that was the only reason why he hadn't simply taken Beloved Anthea and run from this place.

But now they had the standing stone, and the New Meg. They would soon find Constantine and the others. And then they could go.

With or without Marius.

BREAK-IN

"WHY DO WE DO these things?" Finn whispered as they crouched against the outer wall of the manor. Anthea could see his pulse beating wildly at the base of his throat after their climb over the wall followed by a mad dash across the open lawn. She could barely catch her own breath. "These terrible, stupid things?"

"What are you talking about?" Jilly whispered back. "We only do the best things! We are *heroes*."

"Remember that time I helped you sneak out at night, and Keth broke his arm and Anthea got shot?" Finn hissed.

"Remember how you ended up becoming friends with your dear cousin Josephine because of that?" Jilly retorted.

"Both of you be quiet," Anthea whispered, trying not to move her lips, in case that helped to keep the sound down.

Across from them was the standing stone, sitting slightly tilted, jutting out of the middle of the lawn. The only other thing that marred the immaculate gardens was the swath of destruction that led to an outbuilding that had probably once held oxen and carts, or more recently, some of Princess Wilhelmina's motorcars.

This was most definitely the hunting lodge where Prince Adil had been kept. And even though they had gone farther from the palace than they had ever been, they were still on palace grounds. The Imperial Griffin was everywhere: carved in stone atop the wall and into the lintel over the nearest door. Cast in bronze and spewing water from its beak into a large basin in the middle of a flowerbed.

And embroidered on the uniform of the guard who had just taken Meg back inside, after walking her twice, briskly, around the fountain. After which Anthea and the others had made their decision to break in and kidnap her.

Which Finn apparently regretted now.

"We'll be fine," Jilly insisted. "Just give me a boost!"

They were directly below a long window. Most Coronami manor houses had windows that doubled as doors for servants to come and go, but these windows didn't go all the way to the ground. Which was bad and good, as it made it harder to get into the manor, but also easier to be discreet.

This window was just barely over the top of Jilly's head, so she put her knee into Finn's laced fingers, the way she would mount a horse. With her hands gripping the stone window ledge, she carefully raised her head and looked into the room beyond.

"A kind of long parlor or receiving room," she reported. "Empty. Let's go!"

With a groan that was more to do with his misgivings than her weight, Finn straightened so that Jilly was high enough to kneel on the ledge. Anthea was fairly sure that Jilly's beloved silk trousers—already a bit worse for wear after the morning's ride—would not survive this adventure. A shame, really.

Anthea's gown was quite ruined. She had ripped the skirt climbing over the wall, and stained it horribly falling into a muddy flowerbed. No doubt when they returned triumphant with Meg, Queen Josephine would be happy to buy them new wardrobes, and Lady—*Aunt* Cassandra would be delighted to help.

"If I just push right here," Jilly muttered.

There was a squeak, Jilly made a quickly muffled shriek, and then she lurched up and out of view. Anthea clapped a hand to her mouth to keep from shrieking as well, and Finn put an arm across her, pressing them both tightly against the wall so that anyone looking out the window wouldn't see them.

After holding their collective breaths for so long that Anthea was sure she would faint from suspense or lack of oxygen, Jilly's voice came from above them.

"Are you two *cuddling*?" she whispered.

"No!" Finn said, too loudly.

He dropped his arm hastily while Anthea and Jilly both shushed him. Anthea felt her cheeks burning as they turned to look up at Jilly, who was hanging out the window, looking roguish.

"There's no one here, and it's a nice long parlor with three doors," she reported. "One of them leads right to the main hall, and it looks like you can go upstairs to the bedrooms. And there's no one around!"

"But someone is there! There was a guard with Meg!"

But even as she said this, Anthea nudged Finn's shoulder and he cupped his hands to give her a boost.

"But there's no maids running around," Jilly said. "The place feels empty, but not too empty, you know what I mean?"

"No," Finn grunted, raising Anthea up so that Jilly could grab her arms and help pull her onto the ledge.

Anthea was able to get onto the ledge and over with a little more grace than her cousin, despite her skirt. Once inside, she and Jilly both ducked behind a heavy brocade curtain and counted to ten, just in case. When nothing happened, they crept back and Anthea leaned out the window again.

"Be careful," she said to Finn.

"I still think this is foolish," he warned.

"Oh, of course it is," she said, mustering a smile. "But we're going to do it anyway." Then she closed the window, backing into the room.

Anthea looked around. They were in a long gallery or receiving room that ran almost the entire length of the manor. The curtains, wallpaper, and upholstery were all of red brocade, which made for a rather dark room despite the light from the large windows. The heavy wood furniture did nothing to cheer the room, and neither did the wall decorations.

"Are those . . . ?"

"Yes," Jilly said, and led the way to a door at the far end.

Anthea followed her, stumbling on a crease in the carpet as she stared around at the walls. The ceiling was about twenty feet high, and from eight feet from the floor to the ceiling, the walls were decorated with a mosaic made of pistols, arranged in a herringbone pattern and so close together that there was less than a finger's width between them.

"Those are all real?" Anthea said, stumbling again on the edge of the carpet. "There must be thousands of them!"

"They're real," Jilly said. "But the good news is, they're not loaded. Probably." She opened the door a crack and peeped through into the hall. "Just brace yourself, if you thought that was bad."

"What?"

But Jilly had opened the door and slipped out. Anthea followed her and did her best not to squeak or stumble as they made their way into a brightly lit space with a gleaming parquet floor and cream-painted walls entirely covered with . . . rifles, sabers, and spears . . .

This is ridiculous, Anthea thought. *I know it's a hunting lodge, but honestly!*

Beloved?

It's all right, darling, Anthea replied.

She was pleased that Florian could hear her at all. Who even knew what kind of stones had been used in this place? It would be much easier to get out if he could hear her.

Is it you? The voice was anxious and very faint. *Florian's Beloved?*

Anthea stopped dead at the foot of the stairs. Jilly was already partway up, and turned to beckon her to hurry. There were two doors on either side of the hall, and both of them offered a full view of anyone on the stairs.

Anthea almost ran up the stairs, passing her cousin and practically dragging a startled Jilly along with her. At the top of the stairs a tall clock and a throne-like chair provided some cover from below. Anthea hunched behind the chair, still gripping her cousin's arm.

"What is it? Did you see someone?" Jilly whispered, her blue eyes wide.

"The other horses. They are here," Anthea whispered, pointing at the floor. Tears prickled her eyes. "I think I just heard Blossom!"

"Buttercup? Can you . . . ?"

Jilly's face was instantly wet with tears. She clutched at Anthea as though she might fall.

"They must be nearby," Anthea whispered, talking herself through it all. "There was only the one stable or what-have-you outside. They must be in the house itself. The cellar? It was so faint I thought it was Florian at first."

"We have to get them," Jilly said, and started back for the stairs.

Anthea snatched her cousin's arm. "First Meg. We have to, we're so close!"

Jilly nodded reluctantly, and they started down the hall.

They moved as fast as they dared. They crept from door to door, peeping in keyholes. Most of the rooms were empty, with no sign that anyone had occupied them for some time. Anthea was terrified that she would find a room that was occupied . . . by her mother.

She was about to peep through yet another keyhole when she heard a noise from that room. She poked Jilly, who pressed herself against the wall on the other side of the door. Anthea stayed in a crouch, one eye on the keyhole, but ready to run if someone should come out of the room.

She could see a man in the room, but he was standing too close to the door for her to see his face. She could tell that he was wearing a Kronenhofer uniform, however, so she guessed that he was the soldier they had seen guarding Meg outside. Then the man moved, and Anthea saw the princess.

Meg was sitting in a chair at the window, her back to the soldier and therefore the door, but there was no mistaking those proud, straight shoulders and that curly blond hair. Anthea looked up at Jilly and gave a nod, but put her finger to her lips in case her cousin began to celebrate too soon. They needed that soldier out of the room so that they could get Meg, but he was just standing there. Surely he didn't stand inside the room and stare at the girl all day, while she stared out the window?

Anthea beckoned Jilly farther down the hallway so that they could take partial cover behind a wide plinth bearing a marble bust of some heavily bearded Kronenhofer ancestor. She told Jilly what she'd seen, and Jilly asked how close the man had been to the door.

"Why?"

"No reason," Jilly said.

Then she walked right down the corridor to Meg's room and grasped the doorknob. Anthea clapped both hands over her mouth as Jilly silently turned the knob, and then abruptly shoved the door open.

There was a crack and a thud as the soldier fell on his face.

Anthea ran to the door, and she and Jilly jumped over the soldier's prone form to Meg. Her mouth hung open as she looked at them in disbelief, and then with a quickly smothered scream she tipped over her chair to run to them. Anthea wrapped her arms around the younger girl and held her tight while tears poured down both of their faces and Jilly embraced them both.

When the soldier moaned and stirred, Anthea quickly released the princess and closed the door. Clever Meg pulled out a handkerchief and stuffed it into his mouth.

"The curtain ties," Jilly said, snatching them off the curtains.

"Keep watch," Anthea told Meg.

The princess crouched to peek through the keyhole while the two cousins tied up the soldier.

"Mother sent you?" Meg whispered while they worked.

"Yes," Jilly said.

"And your father, too, of course," Anthea added.

"Are they here?" Meg asked tearfully.

"No, they couldn't come," Anthea said.

As she finished the last knot around the man's ankle, she quickly explained that they had to sneak Meg back to the schloss and pretend that she had just arrived on holiday, lest they start a war. Meg gaped at her for a moment.

"Politics," the girl finally hissed.

Anthea and Jilly nodded solemnly. Then they all hugged again.

It took all three of them to drag the unconscious man to the bed and stuff him underneath, pushing with their feet. They kept giggling nervously and trying to hide it. It was pure nerves, and Anthea worried that she might start crying again.

"We have to hurry," Meg said. "They never leave me alone for long. *She* is always popping in." Then she wrinkled her nose and looked guiltily at Anthea.

"My mother *is* here," Anthea said, feeling her stomach drop into her shoes.

"Yes," Meg said. "I'm sorry."

"Then we really need to hurry," Jilly said. "We've got to get the horses and get out of here before Finn blows up the schutzer."

16

Unexpected Help

"BEFORE FINN DOES *WHAT*?" the princess whisper-screamed.

"He's not going to blow it up," Anthea assured Meg. "He's just supposed to see if he can sabotage it a little, so that we can't be followed by that thing."

"Actually, I gave him some matches and told him to blow it up," Jilly said, leading them out of the room.

"Why do you have *matches*?" Anthea demanded. "*Where* do you have matches? You don't even have pockets!"

"I carry matches, a penknife, a needle, and thread at all times," Jilly said primly. "Even when I don't have pockets."

Anthea looked at her cousin's clinging silk suit. She didn't even want to know.

"Do you know the quickest way to get to the horses?" Jilly

asked Meg as they crept back along the corridor to the stairs. "How are they guarded?"

"I've no idea," Meg said. "I haven't been allowed anywhere near them since we were captured. I wasn't sure they were even in the same place until a couple of days ago. But I don't even know where I am! . . . I'm assuming we're in Kronenhof?"

"Yes, only an hour's ride from the imperial schloss," Anthea said with disgust. "Where we have been for over a week now, doing all that we could to find you."

Jilly added, "It hasn't been easy."

Meg gave a little sob. "I'm so . . . so grateful and so . . ."

"No time for that," Jilly said. "We have to get down these stairs and then try and find more stairs."

"They have to be outside," Meg said. "I mean, there has to be a way to get the horses outside."

"Are you sure?" Anthea asked.

"A couple of days ago they started closing my curtains at certain times, and watching me so that I couldn't open them. I think they didn't want me to see the horses out in the garden. The grass looked like it had been trampled a little, off to one side, too. And one of the flowerbeds."

"Brilliant," Jilly said. "Let's just get out of here, then."

Jilly led them back across the hall decorated with spears and knives and rifles, into the red room decorated entirely with pistols. They got the window open; they got Meg out, then Jilly. Arthur flew up from the shrubbery where he had been hiding and landed on the sill just as Anthea started to climb over. His feathers were disarranged, and he was making angry noises. He bit Anthea's shoe.

"Something's wrong," Anthea whispered.

"Clearly—this was too easy," Jilly agreed.

Florian?

Beloved! Shall I come to you? Are you well?

Florian's voice was faint, but Anthea could still hear him.

Constantine is here, Anthea told him. *And the others. We have the New Meg. I am sending her to you. You must carry her quickly to Aunt Cassandra, Mother of Jilly, and none other.*

No! She shall go upon Leonidas! I will not leave!

Very well! Tell him to be ready!

They hadn't really thought all this through. Their plan had simply been to get into the manor, see what they could find, and get out. Finn had wanted to look at the schutzer, and Anthea also agreed with him that they might be keeping the horses in the same outbuilding as the monstrous machine.

Florian, you must try to tell Finn that the others are here in the house, to look for a cellar door. And see if you can speak to Constantine!

I will!

"Move it, bird," Anthea said to Arthur, trying to swing herself over the sill without ruining her dress any further.

But Arthur did not move. He flapped his wings and made more angry noises. Anthea raised her hand to lift him out of the way, force him to fly, and he leaned over and bit her hand.

"Ouch!"

He wasn't biting all that hard, but the action shocked her. When she tried to pry him off with her other hand, she saw that he was gently biting the flesh between her left thumb and forefinger, where she already had a scar from the first time they had met.

"When I rescued you from Constantine," she said aloud.

At the sound of the herd stallion's name, Arthur let go.

"Arthur knows where Constantine is," Anthea told Jilly and Meg, who were both dragging on her feet, frantically trying to get her to join them on the ground.

But Arthur had gone back into the parlor and was marching toward a door on the far side. When he got there, he looked back at Anthea. She held up a finger to tell him to wait, like she would to a person.

"Jilly," she said, climbing all the way back into the room. She leaned out to her cousin and Meg. "Get Meg to the forest. Meg, Leonidas will take you to the palace. Hide in the stable, though."

"I'm not leaving," Jilly said.

"Of course not," Anthea agreed. "But you look for a way into the cellar from the outside, I'm going to follow Arthur around inside."

Jilly nodded. "Let's go!"

Anthea shut the window and followed Arthur to the door. She peeked out carefully, but he just marched down the narrow corridor on the other side and she hurried after.

Although it wasn't as wide or high as the front hall, this was clearly not a servants' passage, either. It was broader than Anthea's outstretched arms, and the walls were papered with green silk and hung with paintings of dogs hunting pheasants and men standing beside dead stags.

"Where are we going?" Anthea whispered.

The doors upstairs had all been closed, but along this corridor they were all open. They passed an office, a small library, and then a room that contained a piano and a harp . . .

And an open window, through which Prince Adil was currently climbing.

"What are you doing here?" Anthea blurted out.

Adil froze. Arthur froze, but then he went to the narrow door at the end of the corridor and scratched it with one talon. Anthea stood in the doorway of the music room, torn between following her owl and finding out why Adil was there.

"Lady Anthea!" He hauled himself through the window and nearly fell on his face. "What are you doing here?"

"I asked you first!"

"I came to find the princess," Prince Adil said. "I tried to tell you where I thought she was, but since I had to write in code, in case it was intercepted, I thought I had better come myself!"

"Have a little faith," Anthea said. She paused. "Though I will admit it took me a little time to decipher!"

"I am sorry," Adil said, crossing the room. "And I didn't know precisely where the hunting lodge was myself until I followed the tracks through the forest today." He peered past her into the hallway, and jumped when he saw Arthur. "What is— Oh, your pet."

"I think he knows where the horses are," Anthea said.

Adil looked astonished. "Is he also . . . magical?"

Anthea let out a little bubble of laughter. "No, he just hates Constantine."

Adil looked confused, but pressed on. "The princess is probably upstairs," he whispered.

"No, she's on her way through the forest," Anthea said. "Are you coming?"

She ignored his surprise, hoping that he would say yes. Not because she particularly wanted him along, but because having him loiter here, or try to sneak away, increased everyone's chances of being caught.

Arthur's scratching was leaving marks on the door and growing louder in the quiet house, too. Anthea didn't have time to wait on the prince. She moved forward and opened the door, scooping up Arthur and plopping him onto her shoulder.

Beyond the door was a wooden staircase that turned sharply downward. This was an area for servants only: there was no carpet, only polished wood floors; and no paintings on the wall, not even wallpaper. A wire nailed along the wall and hung with sporadic electric bulbs provided light. Anthea started down.

Prince Adil followed, quietly closing the door behind him and taking care not to stomp his booted feet on the hard stairs. They went down the turnings, far enough that Anthea was sure they were well below ground. The wall became stone, the temperature dropped, and Anthea prayed that if they did find Con, there would be another way out, because there was no way a horse of his size could go up those stairs.

"There *has* to be another way out," Anthea said aloud when they reached the bottom.

They were in a narrow corridor that ran the length of the manor and was lined with thick oak doors. They were labeled with small brass plaques, and even with her rudimentary grasp of Kronenhofer, Anthea could see that they were doors for vegetables, cheeses, and something along the lines of venison or wild game. It certainly seemed like a good place to store such things: it was cold, and there was a distinct odor. It smelled like . . .

"They're here," Anthea said. She swayed with relief. "Constantine?" she called.

Rage rage fear hunger rage.

Anthea fell to her knees from the weight of Constantine's emotions. And now impressions came from all sides.

Fear hunger sickness terror hunger fear.

"Are you unwell?" Prince Adil tried to raise her to her feet, but Arthur flew at his face and chased him away. "What is it? What is that smell?"

"Open the doors," Anthea gasped. "All the doors."

She struggled to her feet while Prince Adil went to the door marked *Kaese* and tried to open it. It wasn't locked— there was no lock on the door at all—but it opened inward and there was something blocking it. Meanwhile, Anthea lurched down the corridor, past the other doors. At the very end she found what she wanted.

Weinkeller.

Rage rage rage terror hunger rage.

This door had a lock, and Anthea suspected the key that had once been closely guarded by the butler now hung from her mother's waist. Constantine's rage seemed to be singing a duet with Anthea's now. Without thinking she slammed her body against the door, hurting her shoulder and hip, but not caring.

Down the corridor, Prince Adil swore in Kadiji.

He had the door open now. A heap of manure had fallen out onto his feet. It was far ranker than the worst stable smells at Last Farm. Tears poured out of Anthea's eyes as she felt a familiar presence within.

"Brutus!"

But the figure that slowly crept forward was not the stout, stoic animal that had carried Caillin MacRennie so many years. This creature was gaunt. There were sores on his dull hide, and his mane was matted with filth.

Tears completely blinded Anthea. She stumbled back to where Prince Adil stood in shock and, uncaring of the state of the stallion, put her arms around Brutus's sunken neck and sobbed. He flinched when she touched him, but she held on anyway.

Beloved of Florian?

Yes, precious Brutus, we are here to rescue you.

Oh. My Caillin MacRennie? he said feebly.

Is waiting for you at the farm.

Oh.

Anthea whirled to Prince Adil.

"Can you pick a lock? Kick down a door? Get that door at the end open, I don't care how," she ordered. "And then find us a way out!"

She went to the next door, leaving Brutus standing, swaying, half in his filthy cell. Arthur was clinging to her hair and shoulder painfully tight, but she didn't blame him. At the next room, she had to press her full weight against the door to get it open, gagging on the smell that rolled out over them.

"Blossom!"

The mare was on the ground, and if it hadn't been for her labored breathing, Anthea would have thought she was dead. Anthea scrubbed her face with her dirty sleeve and steeled herself.

Get on your feet, Blossom! Right now! Get out of here, we're leaving!

She didn't wait to see, she only hoped that the mare had the strength to get up. She went to the next door.

Campanula! Get out of here, help Blossom! Now! Now!

Campanula's golden chestnut coat was so encrusted that Anthea wouldn't have recognized her had it not been for the tilt of her head as she stood against the far wall of her cell. Campanula had always been a very impudent creature, and some spark of that was still there, to Anthea's relief. The mare was moving for the door before Anthea turned to cross the hallway.

"Buttercup? You better be in here, sweetheart!"

Anthea shouted through the door as she smashed it open with her already sore shoulder. She no longer cared who heard her, if they were found while trying to escape. She was ready to tear the people who had done this apart with her bare hands.

The door flew open suddenly, and Anthea almost fell inside. There was Jilly's beloved mare, covered in sores and filth, her head hanging between her hooves. Anthea could count the mare's ribs. Her cream-colored tail had been chopped off raggedly, and so had her long mane. It was pure cruelty on top of everything else.

Shuffling through the muck in her ruined shoes, Anthea bent and cradled Buttercup's head in her arms, gently raising it up so she could look into the mare's dull eyes.

Come, my beauty, Jilly is waiting outside.

My Jilly . . . and Caesar?

Caesar, too. They came for you. We came to bring you home, my sweet.

"Anthea!" Prince Adil called out sharply, but he hardly needed to warn her.

There was a crash, and a splintering sound, and the door he had been trying to open shattered. Anthea had to let go of Buttercup to run out, just in time to see the prince fall backward onto the floor. Constantine burst out of the wine cellar, looking like a nightmare brought to life.

As filthy and gaunt as the others, he had long bloody streaks on his flanks where he had been whipped. But he was still so massive that his head touched the ceiling of the corridor, and his eyes were bright with such murderous rage that Anthea took a step back into Buttercup's room.

You.

Me, Anthea said, summoning her courage, remembering her own rage. *The Now King waits outside. We have to get Brutus and the mares out. How?*

After what she had seen, Anthea didn't think she could be

shocked again. But she nearly fell over when Constantine gave the merest flick of an ear.

Come. I will show you, he said.

Prince Adil, oblivious to the conversation, had gotten to his feet and was trying to open one of the other doors.

"Is this all of them?"

"Yes," Anthea said.

She put a gentle hand on Buttercup's chin and guided her out into the corridor. Brutus had come all the way out of his cell, and Campanula was in Blossom's cell, nudging the other mare to go out.

"There has to be another door that goes up to the kitchens or something," Prince Adil muttered, dragging on the handle of one of the two doors they hadn't opened. It seemed to be locked.

This way, Constantine said.

The other horses crowded back into their stalls as he passed. They had to: the corridor was too narrow otherwise. Anthea worried that he was going to the stairs—Blossom was too weak to climb them, and Constantine was too big.

But instead he went to a narrow door hidden in the shadows between Brutus's cell and the stairs. It, too, had a plaque. As Anthea hurried to open it, she saw that it was marked *Kohle*.

The door opened easily, and they were in a narrow, dirty room with bins on either side for coal. At the end of the room, where the coal chute should have been, a ramp had been built that went up to a big trapdoor. This was apparently how they had gotten the horses into the cellars, but whether they could get out that way remained to be seen. The ramp was steep, and Anthea couldn't see how to get the door open.

"Let me try," Prince Adil said, carefully edging forward around the horses.

He scrambled up the ramp and crouched at the top to push at the door. It moved a little, and Anthea saw a line of light at one side. The ramp was slippery, and Adil fell and then scrambled back up again.

"There's a rock on top to hold it closed," Adil grunted, bracing his feet and trying again. "I think I can roll it off."

"Here," Anthea said.

She clambered up the ramp and turned, cramming her back against the door. Adil moved so that he was beside her, his own back flattened against the door and his knees nearly touching his ears, the angle was so tight.

Be careful, Beloved of Florian! Buttercup cried out.

Campanula, standing in the corridor, put her head into the room over Blossom's withers. *Footsteps, I hear footsteps!*

"Someone's coming," Anthea told Adil.

"Count of three, then?"

She nodded.

"One. Two. Three!"

They straightened their legs as best they could, heels digging and grinding into the rough wood of the ramp, backs straining against the trapdoor. Anthea could feel the wood bowing around something, something big and heavy. With a scraping sound it shifted, and then fell off the trapdoor with a thud.

Anthea nearly flew out of the chute. Trying to recover she instead slid down into the coal room again. Adil did fall out into the rush of fresh air and sunshine. But he got to his feet and Anthea heard him heave the trapdoor away as she eased down to the floor and took hold of Brutus's mane. Constantine was standing at the front, but she didn't dare to lay a hand on him.

He hardly needed any urging, however, but picked his way carefully up the ramp and out the open hole. Anthea clucked to Brutus and sent him up on Con's heels. Buttercup was next, shaking from illness or hunger or fear or all three. Anthea grasped the choppy remains of Buttercup's mane and walked up with her, slowly and just as uncertainly. Both of them slipped on the splintery wood as they went. At the top she found Adil standing on the lawn, fidgeting under the weight of Constantine's scrutiny.

"What do I do?" Adil whispered.

They were on the far side of the manor now. There was no sign of the standing stone, or the gate they had come through. Or Jilly or Finn. Or Florian. And there was no way that they could get an entire herd of slow, sick horses around the bulk of the manor in broad daylight without being spotted.

"Where's the front gate?" Anthea said.

"The *front* gate?"

"We came through the *other* side," she said. "We have to get them into the forest, fast! Can you lead them out the nearest gate?"

"The front gate?" he repeated.

"Well, they won't be expecting that," she managed to joke.

She looked Con in the eyes. *King of horses, herd stallion of Leana,* she said with great formality. *You don't like me, but I don't care. Listen to me anyway. This is Adil, Prince of the Men of Kadij. He has been to this place before. Follow him out. The Now King is here. Florian is here. Go!*

I will wait for the mares, he said in his harsh voice that made Anthea's ears feel scraped on the inside.

"All right," Anthea said. "Let me get the last two, but then we need to move quickly!"

She called out to Florian, but there was no response. She hoped that meant he was far on the other side of the standing stone, and not because he had left her entirely. They would need everyone's help, human and horse, to get the rescued horses through the woods.

The explosion came right as Anthea slid back down the chute. It knocked her sideways off the ramp, and she hit her bruised hip on a coal bin, giving a sharp cry of pain and surprise.

What is it? Brutus sounded near to panicking.

Beloved of Florian? Are you damaged? Buttercup was definitely panicking.

I'm fine! Just fine! Anthea assured them. *Let's get out of here!*

The second explosion came as Anthea was getting to her feet, and threw her against Blossom. The mare cried out as Anthea fell on the sores that marred her once-beautiful coat.

"What is happening?"

Anthea couldn't help but say it aloud. Was Finn really trying to blow up the schutzer? Couldn't he have waited until they were clear? But if she could get the two mares up the ramp, the explosion would provide a distraction for them. She gently took hold of Blossom's mane.

"Anthea Genevia Thornley, you have ruined that dress!"

Anthea froze.

"You've never been the most tidy young lady, but honestly, this is beyond anything! It looks like an old cleaning rag!"

Still gripping Blossom's mane, Anthea turned very slowly and looked over Blossom's back, past Campanula, to the narrow doorway of the coal room. There stood her mother, stylishly clad in an embroidered shirtwaist with a navy blue skirt, a natural-colored straw hat perched atop her upswept hair adorned with three red silk roses. Elegant, understated, and with a pistol pointed at her daughter.

"Oh, hello, Mother," Anthea said, as coolly as she could. "I wondered when you would turn up."

CAPTURED

"SO BOLD!" HER MOTHER laughed. "It reminds me of your father! Dear Charles!" She shook her head, but her pistol never wavered. "My poor Custard was such an optimist, too. I see he passed that on to you. The very idea that you could just waltz right into the private hunting lodge of the emperor of Kronenhof and steal a herd of horses and a hostage princess? Armed with what? Your wits, your cousin, a pair of handsome boys, and an *owl*?"

"More or less," Anthea said, still trying to keep her tone cool.

Beloved of Florian? Blossom's voice was as shaky as Anthea's was trying not to be. *If we run? Will she shoot us?*

She will. Don't run.

Anthea reached out her other hand to Campanula and

repeated the instruction. The bigger mare leaned into her hand, her stubborn nature put aside for once. Anthea couldn't imagine how awful it would be to smell freedom and have it taken away again.

Or maybe she did know.

"Are you telling them not to move?" Her mother raised a plucked eyebrow, nodding her head at the mares. "Very smart."

The only thing Anthea could do was buy the others more time to escape. She reached out to the bramble hedge that was Constantine's mind.

Run. Run now. My mother has caught us. I will stay with the mares. I will find a way to get them out safely. You have to take the others, find Finn, and go.

I will not! I will not leave mares behind!

You will, Anthea shouted, making her mental voice like a whip cracking. *You will leave two mares behind so that the rest of the herd will live!*

You do not order me around!

Beloved?

Florian, run! Anthea screamed in her mind.

If Constantine wouldn't listen, perhaps Florian would. She ordered him to go as loudly as she could. The mares stirred, disturbed, and Campanula turned to face Anthea's mother and took up a defensive stance.

We go, Constantine said suddenly.

Good! Protect the Now King and the New Meg! Anthea shouted.

We will return.

I know!

"Come along now, Anthea," her mother said, gesturing with the pistol. "Put these creatures back in their stalls."

Anthea felt like the spiky coal of Constantine's rage had lodged in her heart. She turned on her mother, wondering if flames could actually explode from her eyes.

"These aren't stalls. They're cells. Prison cells," Anthea snarled. "Look at them! Knee deep in filth! Sick, starving, wounded!"

"So dramatic!" Her mother rolled her eyes. "It's not like we had a stable to keep them in! We're doing the best we can!"

"I highly doubt that."

Her mother laughed. "All right! We're *not* taking good care of them. Because we don't actually care what happens to them."

Anthea gaped at her mother. "Then why . . . why did you kidnap them?"

"I am not going to stand here in this malodorous cellar and discuss it," her mother said, as though Anthea had chosen the location.

Anthea snorted.

"You've been spending too much time with these animals," Genevia said, wincing. "Now come along."

Anthea put one arm over Blossom's back, the other over Campanula's. It wasn't very comfortable, since the backs of both mares were higher than her shoulders, but that didn't matter. She stared at her mother.

"No."

"I beg your pardon?"

"You heard me. You don't want the horses, so I'm taking them and going."

"So like your father," her mother said.

She raised her pistol and pointed it directly between Campanula's eyes. She pulled back the hammer and braced her wrist with her other hand.

"What are you doing?" Anthea couldn't keep the tremor out of her voice.

"I'm not going to discuss it here," Genevia said. "Honestly, if Wilhelm would say the word, I'd end them all. They're only taking up room, making filth, causing problems. But at least they served some purpose, now that we've got you."

The emphasis on "you" was not lost on Anthea. They hadn't recaptured Meg, then. Her mother would surely have thrown that in her face.

"If you want me, you have to keep them alive," Anthea said shakily. "I'll . . . I'll run away. Or jump in front of the gun."

Nobody moved for a minute, two minutes. Even the horses barely breathed. Finally Genevia released the hammer.

"So like your father," she said. Her tone was neutral, and Anthea couldn't tell if that was good or bad in her mother's eyes. "Come along. Leave the horses. We have nowhere else to put them, and two of them can't do any mischief having the run of the cellars." Genevia went out of the coal room.

Go up the ramp! Run! Anthea said at once.

"Don't even think about ordering them outside," her mother called back.

As if on cue, a thud came from the top of the ramp, and it went dark in the coal room. There was another thud as the rock was replaced atop the trapdoor. Genevia stepped back into the room.

"Perhaps, after we figure out how you got onto the grounds, we can allow you to take them into the gardens for some air and sunlight. We've been trying, but they're so intractable! But for now: leave them."

Anthea stumbled after Genevia, putting herself between the mares and her mother. Genevia already had a hand on the door to the stairs. She had one eyebrow raised and looked seconds away from tapping her foot in impatience.

Doing her best to ignore her mother, Anthea turned to Campanula and gently held the mare's face so that she could look her in the eyes.

You are brave and strong, she said. *I must go upstairs, but I will be here, in this place, with you, until we are all free. I will make sure that you have food, fresh water. I will have this place cleaned. I will take you to graze on the grass. But you must be calm. You must be quiet. You must take care of Blossom.*

I will do this, Anthea Bluebell's Companion, Campanula said. *I will be as a mother to Blossom.*

Anthea did not know how the mares organized themselves, but there was an emphasis on "mother" that made Anthea think Campanula meant it in a stronger sense of the word than Anthea would have thought. Even though they were subjects of the herd stallion, Anthea knew from Florian that the mares had names they used only among themselves, and a hierarchy that even Constantine had no say in.

Thank you, good Campanula, Anthea said, before turning and taking up Blossom's drooping head.

Sweet girl, she said. *I know that you are ill, and scared, but you have been so good! I need you to keep on being good. I need you to hang on. I will go upstairs now, but I will not leave this place without you. I swear it! Campanula will be as a mother to you, and together we will get you out!*

Where is My Meg? Blossom said plaintively. *I thought she was here!*

She was *here, sweetheart! But she had to go, just a little ways away. To be safe. I will bring you to her. Soon.*

"Come along!"

Anthea gave the mares each a final caress and then followed her mother up the endless turning stair into the light and air of the manor house proper. There was a footman waiting there, completely unfazed by Anthea's bedraggled appearance. He led them up the stairs to a room next to the one where Meg had recently been.

Anthea's heart was pounding. Did her mother know that Meg had gotten free? Did she even wonder about the explosions outside?

"I'll have to loan you some of my things," Genevia said when the footman had left the room. "There's a bathroom just there." She pointed to the door beside the wardrobe. "Wash up; I'll bring you a fresh gown. Then we'll talk."

"I want to see Meg first," Anthea said, her heart in her throat. "I want to make sure she's all right."

There was a long pause. Anthea did her best to look at her mother directly, and not let her eyes wander toward the wall her room shared with Meg's. Genevia never looked away, but she was the first to break the silence.

"Very nice," she said. "Good tone, good use of eye contact." She smiled. "We'll make a Rose Maiden out of you yet!"

Genevia turned to leave.

"What do you mean? Where is Meg?"

"I assume she's wherever your friends took her, before they set fire to the old ox stable," Genevia said without looking at her daughter. She shut and locked the door behind her.

Anthea ran to the window. She could see the standing stone, the lawns, a fountain . . . and nothing else. Even if she opened the window and leaned out she wouldn't be able to see around the corner of the mansion to the ox stable or the gate where the schutzer had come in and the horses had presumably gone out.

There was no sign of anyone, and nothing out of the ordinary at all. Meg was gone; her mother surely would have gloated if any of the others had been captured. But it was strange that, after going to the work of abducting the princess and keeping her for weeks, her mother didn't care that she was free.

Anthea unlatched the window and sat on the sill.

Florian? Florian, my love?

Nothing. Whether it was the standing stone, the rocks in the wall, or that he was too far away, Anthea didn't know. The only horses she could sense were the two mares down in the cellar. She sent them reassuring thoughts and closed the window.

Her mother might be evil, but she was also right: Anthea was filthy from head to toe. She stripped off her ruined things and went to take a bath.

CONSTANTINE

Florian's human filly had not lied. Here was the Now King, emerging from the burning stable. Constantine felt great pride seeing how he had grown taller, stronger, and fiercer in the time that Constantine had been gone. And now he had destroyed that evil machine The Woman of Dead Roses had used to tear down the Last House and uproot the stone that caused such confusion.

The Now King, with great nobility, ordered them all into the woods, leaping up easily to ride behind the Meg filly on Leonidas. The welts on Constantine's back were too raw to allow the king to ride, and this put strength into Constantine's weakened limbs, as though distancing himself from the place of his beating would distance him from the pain.

Florian did not want to leave his human filly, but the Now

King insisted. Constantine gave the order, so Florian had no choice but to come, sulking, at the rear of their herd, behind She Who Was Jilly and the other herd members. His behavior was foolish and stubborn, and Constantine would have words to say to him when they arrived at the safe place that the Now King had promised.

Where that safe place could be Constantine did not know. They had not the strength to go very far, and he could not imagine that anyplace within easy riding of The Woman of Dead Roses could be safe. But he trusted the Now King. Although he was young, he would never lead them into danger.

18

A Proposition

THE NEXT DAY ANTHEA found herself sitting across from her mother in the parlor of the hunting lodge. After threatening her earlier, Genevia had gone on to discuss the new, shorter skirt lengths and how well they looked on Anthea. She had also asked Anthea about her education at the Last Farm, wanting to know Miss Ravel's credentials and her teaching methods. She had mused about having Anthea spend one final year at Miss Miniver's Rose Academy in Travertine, as though she had any say in her daughter's education.

Anthea couldn't take it anymore. They were expecting the emperor for tea at any moment, and this looked like her only chance to get answers. "Oh, stop this ridiculous small talk, Genevia," she snapped, interrupting her midsentence.

"I dislike both your tone and your use of my given name, young lady," Genevia replied, smoothing her dress.

"I'm not going to call you *Mother*," Anthea said with a snort. "Why on earth would I? When have I ever been your daughter?"

She couldn't help but think of all the ways her real mother failed her, and all the ways others had acted more like a mother than Genevia ever did. Queen Josephine, so intelligent and kind, caring for Anthea like her own daughter when she arrived bloodied and ill on her doorstep. Aunt Cassandra, terrified of horses, holding Florian's head while Anthea bandaged him after his accident.

And sitting in front of Anthea was her own mother, smug and smiling, always acting as though she were the most beautiful, the most clever woman in the world. As though her schemes were too complex, too mysterious, to ever be revealed, when in reality all she desired was power, and her solution to anything that got in her way was to kill it. Anthea wondered for a wild moment if her mother had somehow arranged for the train to derail, when she was tired of being married.

"I want to know, right now, what *is* your endgame, Genevia?" Anthea asked coldly. "You tried to drive a wedge between King Gareth and Josephine, and that appears to have failed. You tried to get horses blamed for an epidemic you started . . . and that failed, though it did kill thousands of people. And why? What do *you* want?"

"A throne," Genevia said simply. "You said it yourself: I couldn't get rid of that insipid Josephine . . . though I did try!"

"I never said insipid," Anthea muttered. She didn't dare to speak any louder, for fear that she would disrupt Genevia's confession.

"And then I realized," Genevia went on, "Gareth's an idiot. Coronam is practically on the edge of the world . . . there are better places! Places where fools wouldn't kill the horses but use them, with my help. No horse can defeat the schutzerlei, but properly used the animals could be the symbol that Kronenhof needs to truly elevate their empire!"

"If anyone else in the world said they wanted a horse I would be beside myself with joy," Anthea said coldly. "I saw what you did. And that's *after* you kidnapped them!"

"What *I* did?" Genevia's tone was gently baffled, mildly offended.

"Do *not* pretend innocence," Anthea said, her voice coming out much lower and harsher than either of them was expecting. "Even you know exactly what you did to these horses. So tell me." Anthea paused, steeling herself. "Why kidnap these horses when you couldn't be bothered to feed them? To take care of them at all?"

Genevia rolled her eyes. "The Kronenhofer have failed spectacularly at that, haven't they? You'll notice that there are no ghost stallions, after what they did. So we'll need you to stay and teach people here how to care for horses."

Anthea felt a queasy lurch in her midsection. She gaped back at her mother. *Stay?*

"That's right," Genevia said, watching her closely. "You stay here. With Florian. And the mare. Perhaps they will have adorable little foals together. Perhaps breeding them with the local horses will produce more impressive results."

"Or what?" Anthea said, playing her one bargaining chip. "If I say no, if I leave, if you get rid of me somehow, you'll have *nothing*."

"That's very true," Genevia said. "But think about what you'll have if you stay. Your precious horses. A position in the palace. An emperor for a stepfather."

Anthea shuddered.

Genevia's face hardened.

"You've never understood what it's like, being powerless," Genevia said in a hard voice. "Coming from some awful little village, your only hope that you'll catch the notice of some foolish queen, or an even more foolish man, and they'll throw you some scraps. I had to fight, to claw, my way to everything I have! Then I almost lost everything I had worked for over Charles and that stupid farm! Lucky for me that cow decided to lie down on the train tracks that day and caused the accident!"

Anthea felt the words like a blow. So it really had been an accident, but how could her mother be so cavalier about the death of her husband!

Genevia went on, oblivious to Anthea's pain. "I wanted better for you. I made sure that you had all the best Coronam had to offer: raised in Travertine, the finest Rose Academy training. I wanted you ready to join me as soon as I reached my goal!"

"Of . . . what? Marrying a foolish king?" Anthea said, then wished she could take the words back when she saw the near-crazed look in her mother's eyes.

"An *emperor*," Genevia snarled. "Think this through, Anthea. With the backing of both Josephine and Wilhelm, your dear friend Finn could take his place on the throne of Leana. Do you want to go home, tail between your legs? Or do you want to be the one who stands at the right hand of an emperor? The one who returned a princess safely to her mother, earning the gratitude of Coronam? The one who gave a heroic boy king the crown he had been denied?"

"And if I don't want to play the hero?" Anthea said.

"Then your friends won't leave the palace alive," her mother said simply.

19

HIS BEARDED
IMPERIAL MAJESTY

"WE WILL BE PLEASED to host Princess Margaret of Coronam at the palace," Emperor Wilhelm said.

He was sitting with his back to one of the broad windows of the manor's parlor so that he was haloed with light. It had only been a few minutes since Genevia's ultimatum, and Anthea's mind was racing. She could barely focus on the words coming out of his mouth.

"When you and your mother have finished getting caught up, you must rejoin us," he continued. "My daughter is pleased to have so many ladies to keep her company. I am hoping that some of Lady Cassandra's . . . and of course your . . . excellent manners will rub off on her. Perhaps she will give up this mania for motorcars and pay a little more attention to balls and dancing!"

The emperor chuckled, leaning back at ease. And why shouldn't he be? It was his chair. In his hunting lodge. Just a stone's throw from his schloss.

Anthea, sitting rigid on the edge of the sofa, stared at him. She opened her mouth to speak and then closed it again. She felt trapped. If she left Kronenhof, Genevia would have her friends killed.

"We understand her wish to travel incognito for a little while," the emperor continued, "but it shows good breeding on her part that she has ended this folly and chosen to finish her journey with an official state visit to us."

Anthea felt dizzy. This was the exact story that Queen Josephine had instructed them to tell: that Meg was traveling abroad with a few close friends, and would soon return to public life. But Anthea hadn't expected the emperor to know this story, let alone go along with it. When they found Meg, the plan had been to slip her into the palace and approach the good-natured Fritz or even Wilhelmina first, assuming that they didn't know about Meg's abduction. Emperor Wilhelm would have to go along with it, lest he look foolish in front of the court.

And now he was reciting his lines perfectly. Or rather, Anthea's lines.

Actually, they were supposed to be Lady Cassandra's lines. Anthea had a sudden picture of her aunt hustling Meg into a bath and then finding her some clothes to wear, humming under her breath as she laid out gowns. Her dogs would be rolling around on the rug, getting stepped on.

Tears started in Anthea's eyes. The longing to be there . . . to be anywhere but where she was, became almost a physical pain. She had to breathe deeply before she replied.

"I'm so glad that Meg is safely at the schloss," Anthea said. "We have been so worried about her, leaving as suddenly as she did."

Anthea felt a trickle of sweat run down her back. She hoped that she sounded calm enough, that her words were vague enough. She did not want to anger the emperor, or worse, her mother.

She shifted a little on the sofa, trying surreptitiously to adjust her gown. It was one of her mother's, navy blue with red roses around the square neckline, and fit her badly.

"I'm sure you are anxious to rejoin your companions," Genevia said. It was a cruel reminder of what was at stake.

She poured tea for the three of them, and offered around a plate of sandwiches. Anthea started to reach for the butter biscuits, to crumble one up for Arthur, when she remembered that he was down in the cellars with the mares.

They were still knee deep in filth, but they had fresh water and food, and both of these things were hanging from hooks on the wall to keep them clear of the dirt. Anthea had checked on them last night and again this morning, in between the horrible conversation with her mother and pretending that everything was completely normal.

Anthea honestly wondered if her mother had gone mad.

She was hosting the emperor of Kronenhof for tea, as though they were in her own parlor. Genevia had introduced the emperor as though Anthea had not been living in the palace for nearly two weeks. When Emperor Wilhelm had pointed this out, with a jovial air that Anthea had never seen before, her mother had laughed.

"Silly me! I nearly forgot that she came here with my sister-in-law . . . Cassandra, you know, not Deirdre!" Genevia winked broadly. "Though I suppose that's still a secret? And speaking of Deirdre, are she and Daniel still there? He's such a stuffed shirt, you're an angel for putting up with him, Anthea!"

"I would like to rejoin my friends," Anthea said carefully to keep her voice from wavering. "And of course, dear Meg. I have not seen her in some time."

"Simple enough," Emperor Wilhelm said. "It's an easy drive from here to the palace gates. Or I suppose you could ride one of the horses."

"The mares here are not well," Anthea said. "I would like to move them immediately to the more luxurious accommodations that you provided at the schloss." She summoned a smile. "But I will have to walk them there very slowly."

"Of course," the emperor said. "Whatever you need, just ask for it."

"That's so generous of you, Wilhelm," Genevia said.

"It seems only fair," Emperor Wilhelm said, exchanging a look with Genevia.

Anthea closed her eyes for just a moment. The emperor was involved, not only in lying about the kidnapping, but in holding Anthea hostage now. She could see it in his face. Of course he was; Anthea wasn't sure why she thought otherwise. But one question still lingered.

"If I may," she began, "I have been most curious as to why my dear mother brought Constantine and the others here to Kronenhof."

She almost managed a little laugh, decided it was too risky, and settled on a politely interested smile that Miss Miniver would have given her top marks for.

"You've seen the ghosts in the forest, I think?" Emperor Wilhelm said.

"I—I have," Anthea replied, startled at this sudden turn in the conversation.

She wondered suddenly if Marius had found his way to the ghosts, and if he was all right. She hoped that, even with Constantine to care for, Finn made the time to look for poor Marius.

"So you know that we Kronenhofer are not afraid of horses," Emperor Wilhelm said.

Anthea felt her scarred eyebrow arch. She remembered the look on the face of the soldier who had told her about the "ghosts." Perhaps Wilhelm was not, but some of his people definitely were.

"Our horses are not like yours. We do not have the Way here." He grimaced. "I tried, time and again, to tame the creatures. The results were not promising."

Anthea just nodded, very aware of her mother's eyes on her face. Genevia and the emperor clearly did not realize that the same stone that they hauled all the way from Coronam was littered throughout the Kronenhofer forest . . . And they weren't going to find out from Anthea!

"It's clear," Genevia said, "that King Gareth is never going to harness the potential of the horses." She sounded disappointed. "Even when Josephine, of all people, turned out to be an advocate for them . . . and a secret Leanan!"

Emperor Wilhelm was shaking his head. "A very strange situation," he said. "To have such secrets in one's own house!"

"But His Imperial Majesty was very interested in finding out what capabilities the horses might have," Genevia purred, smiling at Emperor Wilhelm. "Despite his having much more advanced weapons than Coronam, he is still willing to explore new modes of communication and warfare by utilizing the horses."

"So you . . . brought the herd stallion here?"

Anthea did her best not to use words like "kidnap" or "nearly kill."

"Obviously we needed the most powerful stallion, in order

to establish our own herd here, and begin training them to work with us," Emperor Wilhelm said.

"You have to have cannons and schutzers *and* horses?" Anthea blurted out.

Wilhelm smiled grimly. "The might of Kronenhof knows no boundaries." His face darkened, and he flicked a glance at Genevia. "But we did not anticipate that the creatures would be so difficult to work with. That all of them would be so stubborn, and violent."

Violent? Anthea, who had nearly been killed by Constantine once herself, wondered how many Kronenhofer soldiers had been injured, or even died. She knew that she should feel sorry for them; after all, they were just carrying out orders. It wasn't their fault that the people giving the orders were evil.

"It seems that you have had incidents with this stallion yourself," Emperor Wilhelm said, watching her carefully. "So you know of his nature."

"Indeed I do," Anthea said. "At the farm, only Uncle Andrew or Finn care for him, and only Finn can ride him."

"Yes, quite a problem," Genevia said. "Or so we thought."

Anthea twitched her sleeves. It felt like someone had just dragged an icy fingernail down her spine beneath her ill-fitting gown.

"Having had time to observe the other horses you brought with you," Emperor Wilhelm said, "we believe that Florian would be a much more suitable stallion for the emperor of Kronenhof to ride."

Anthea burst out laughing. It was one thing to force Anthea to stay in Kronenhof, but it was another thing entirely to allow the emperor to ride Florian. Her Florian!

"Anthea!" Genevia's voice and face were equally shocked. "Apologize!"

Anthea's laughter died away immediately. She looked up to see that the emperor was livid. He turned to her mother, rising from his seat.

"I am tired of these children and their foolishness," he said.

Anthea rose. She thought her legs would shake, but in reality she felt too numb, almost as though she were floating away from her body. She wished that she could fly, gathering the horses in her arms, and soar back to the Last Farm.

"I will not apologize," Anthea said to Genevia. She felt as though her voice was coming from very far away. "It is quite clear that you do not understand anything, despite being Leanan and having lived among horses."

She turned to the emperor, hoping to appeal to him since her mother was either mad, or evil, or both.

"Sire, forgive me for not taking the time to explain this all to you much sooner. The connection between horse and rider is very deep, and can't be forced. Florian and I have been bonded since he was born and I was little more than a baby myself. You might very well have the Way, but in order for us to test that, you would have to spend time with horses who do not have a rider, and see if you could form a rapport with them. The horses that my mother kidnapped—"

Out of the corner of her eye, Anthea saw her mother make a jerky movement at the word, but she continued nonetheless.

"The horses that my mother kidnapped," she repeated, louder, "all have riders. The bond between the herd stallion and the Leanan royal family is especially important. Constantine would only allow Finn to touch him after he deemed Finn worthy of riding a herd stallion."

"But Finn rode your Florian in that foolish race," Emperor Wilhelm said. "And you have another horse you ride—two in fact! So it's time for you to stop this little act that only you special children can use these horses. I have spent a great deal of time with Florian when you are not there. I see how he commands the others. I will take him. I will take them all, and with Florian at their head, we will start a new army. More nimble and silent than the schutzerlei, faster and stronger than infantry. No other nation will be able to stand against us."

Anthea stood in silence, then turned and walked out of the room. They could keep her in Kronenhof, but they couldn't keep her in this manor one second longer.

She walked down the hallway, to the stairs, and went down to the cellars. She dimly heard her mother calling her, but Genevia didn't chase her, so Anthea didn't stop. A footman stepped between her and the door to the cellars, but he looked at her expression and stepped back.

Anthea went down the stairs at a marching pace that she didn't have to think about. Because she couldn't think about anything except getting out. The numb feeling had not left her body, but she kept going nonetheless.

At the bottom of the stairs Arthur was waiting, looking like a rock in the dim light in the middle of the cellar corridor.

"We're leaving," Anthea said to him.

He hooted and flew up to her shoulder. Both mares came out of the room marked *Kaese*. They looked slightly better, and Anthea was no longer concerned that Blossom might die at any moment.

Snapping her fingers for them to follow, Anthea went into the coal room and surveyed the ramp. She sat on it and backed her way up, feeling a sense of satisfaction when her shoe caught in the hem of her borrowed skirt and she heard it rip. At the top of the ramp, she braced her back against the trapdoor and heaved, nearly falling out of the chute when the door moved easily. There was no rock weighing it down today.

Either they didn't think she would try again, or they didn't care.

Before she could slide down to guide them, Campanula started up the ramp on her own, Blossom right on her heels. Anthea scrambled out of the way as they took the steepest part in a rush, and then cradled both of their heads to her breast while they got their breath.

Anthea waved jauntily to the gardener who stood gaping at her as she led the mares across the lawn toward the wide gate. It would take hours to get back, with the mares in such poor condition, but at least the weather was fine.

When Anthea got to the gate, she found that it had been broken and was hanging drunkenly off its hinges.

"Well, that's one blessing," Anthea said. "Two, I suppose, if you count the rock being gone."

"And you're *welcome*," Finn said, coming out of the trees. "I nearly dislocated my shoulder moving it!"

"Finn!"

He grinned. "I thought you might need a ride back to the palace."

A shadow moved out from the trees.

Beloved?

My darling!

CONFESSIONS

WHEN THE DOOR TO the makeshift stable on the palace grounds opened, Anthea reined in Florian and reached for a pistol that wasn't there. She still couldn't believe that she and Finn hadn't been followed. Of course, Genevia knew exactly where she was going—the only place she could go, now, without endangering her friends.

She half expected to be met at the palace grounds by a guard, but it was Aunt Cassandra who came rushing out of the stable. The elegant Rose Matron was almost disheveled: gown creased and strands of curling brown hair coming down from her coiffure.

Her face lit up when she saw Anthea sitting on Florian, and Anthea threw herself off his back and into Aunt Cassandra's embrace. She buried her face in her aunt's shoulder and sobbed while Cassandra stroked her hair and murmured that it was all right, everything would be all right now.

Jilly came out and lunged at Anthea, hugging her and her mother together. Finn took the other horses into the stable while they hugged and cried, except for Florian, who stood nearby and nibbled at Anthea's hair every now and then.

Which just made Anthea cry harder.

"Oh, Thea! What did she do to you?" Jilly managed to gently pry Anthea off Aunt Cassandra and looked into her eyes. "Tell us! What happened?"

Anthea couldn't. She couldn't say anything in front of Florian. She was afraid to even think it.

"Is Meg all right?" she asked instead. "And Constantine and the others? We have to take care of Campanula and Blossom. What have you done for the others?"

Anthea took Florian's reins and led him into the now-cramped quarters for the horses. Constantine had been put in the very first stall, keeping watch over the door. Anthea flinched when she nearly walked right into his head. He pulled back just in time, but he didn't challenge her or Florian, simply watched them go by.

Did you explain to Constantine that you had to be the herd stallion in this place until we found him? Anthea asked Florian nervously.

Yes, of course, Florian said. *And I said to him that now that he had returned, I would step back into my proper place.*

And?

All is well, Florian assured her. *But are you sure that you are well?*

I am fine, Anthea said firmly.

"We'll need to clean them first, gently," Anthea said aloud.

"Oh, it's been awful," Jilly said, coming into the stable and heading immediately for the stall now shared by Bluebell and Buttercup.

Beautiful Buttercup was far too thin, and being washed had revealed the sores on her legs from standing in her own muck for so long. There were scissors and a comb laid on top of an overturned bucket, and Jilly had apparently been in the middle of trimming her mane to make it lie evenly when they arrived.

Or so Anthea thought. But to her astonishment, it was Aunt Cassandra who took up the scissors and began gently snipping at the tattered mane, while Jilly held Buttercup's head and looked on. Bluebell had her neck lying over Buttercup's back, watching, but she raised her head to look at Anthea.

I am glad that you are well, she said.

Thank you. Anthea felt her eyes begin to prickle again. *I am . . . I am so glad that you were never taken! I am so glad that I don't have to see you like this!*

She waved a hand at Campanula and Blossom, who took up the remaining stall. Finn was walking around them, rubbing his face in an exhausted gesture, trying to decide how to get started.

"We need to tell Meg that Blossom is here," Anthea said. She saw Blossom's ears flicker, and was glad to see any interest from the downtrodden mare. "And how is Meg?" she asked again.

"Meg is being the perfect princess," Jilly said. "At the schloss, wearing one of my more boring gowns . . . every inch the proper young lady."

"Are my aunt and uncle still here?" Anthea asked.

During the ride back, Finn had assured her that they had all reached the schloss safely. But she had not been in the mood to talk. Not even to Florian.

"Yes, and I think we need to keep an eye on that situation," Jilly said darkly. "Little Begonia Rose looked like she'd just been offered a platter of sweets when she was introduced to a real live princess. I had to leave the room before I vomited from the amount of fawning!"

"Of course she wants to befriend a princess," Aunt Cassandra said. "She's angling for a position at court! She'd be foolish to pass up this opportunity with Meg—Princess Margaret." Cassandra stepped back and frowned, then made a few more snips. "And you know very well that her name is Belinda Rose, not Begonia. Or Bettina. Or Bathilda . . . which isn't actually a name."

"Oh, but it's so much more fun," Jilly said. "It used to make

Thea all defensive, until she learned to let her hair down." She smiled brightly at Anthea. "And now it's fun watching to see if Brunhilda Rose will correct me or just smile politely."

"Brunhilda?" Anthea felt a smile twitch the corners of her own mouth.

"I haven't used that one to her face yet," Jilly said. "What do you think? Is it too much?"

"It's a Kronenhofer name," Finn said judiciously. "I can see where you could make that mistake."

"Finn! Don't encourage her," Aunt Cassandra scolded.

She was laughing, however, as she moved around to look at Buttercup's tail. Buttercup shook her short mane, and Anthea stroked her nose, relieved to see the mare perking up.

Anthea just busied herself taking Florian's tack off and putting it away. She rubbed him down briskly, doing her best not to cry. She let the banter between Jilly and Finn wash over her, and exchanged looks with Jilly over Aunt Cassandra's fussing about with the horses, petting them and offering to trim the tangled parts of the newly rescued horses' manes and tails.

Does my aunt Cassandra have the Way? Anthea dared to ask Florian, figuring that it was a topic that wouldn't make her red and swollen eyes tear up again.

No, Florian said. *But there is a light in her, a kindness. Very different from the others here,* he added.

I know, Anthea replied. *We will go home soon.*

We have the herd stallion, and Brutus and the mares, and the New Meg, Florian said. *That is why we came . . . we can leave soon, can't we?*

Soon, was all she could say.

Beloved, what is wrong?

"Blossom!" Meg screamed from the door of the stable. "My angel! What did they do to you?"

The princess flew to the stall that held Blossom and Campanula and climbed under the bar that they were using for a gate. Without a care for her crisp blue-and-white-striped morning gown, she threw her arms around the neck of the still-filthy Blossom and kissed the mare's nose. Then she turned and embraced Campanula.

"And you took care of her? Thank you so much!" Meg said to the other mare.

"We're just going to start cleaning them," Finn said. "Now they've had a bite to eat."

"I'll take care of Blossom," Meg said. "Campanula, too, since you're all busy."

"Campanula? That sounds like a skin disease," said Princess Wilhelmina from the doorway.

Everyone froze, but just for a moment. Lady Cassandra recovered very quickly, and put her scissors aside to greet the princess formally. Meg waved to her as though they were across a garden.

"So kind of you to come and see how the horses are all faring," Lady Cassandra said.

"This is Blossom, my particular favorite," Meg said, almost on top of Cassandra's words. "The one I was just telling you about!"

"I still don't understand how you *lost* a herd of horses," Princess Wilhelmina said, coming all the way into the stable. "I mean, how did they get across the ocean? Did they swim?"

"It's like I told your brother," Jilly said. "Something happened right after we arrived here, and they bolted. Fortunately they found their way to the forest, and we were able to track them down at last!"

Anthea was more than a little impressed that Jilly had managed to remember their story and recite it so convincingly.

"Ugh, they look awful," Princess Wilhelmina said, wrinkling her nose. "And what happened to that other stallion? The one you always rode, but didn't race?" she asked Finn.

Another awkward silence. Finn and Constantine were clearly deep in conversation, or more likely: Constantine was trying to order Finn to do or say something and Finn was arguing with the herd stallion.

"He has to be kept at a distance," Anthea heard herself saying. "Marius was the herd stallion while Constantine was missing. Now we have to keep them separated so that they won't fight for dominance." She breathed heavily through her nose. "We made a little pen for him in the forest," she added.

"Just for a few days," Finn said. "We need to slowly

reintroduce the stallions, to reestablish the hierarchy. It's very important for herds to have a solid structure."

"What about this one?" Princess Wilhelmina pointed at Florian.

"He's the herd's second in command," Finn said easily.

Princess Wilhelmina looked around at them. Anthea in her torn and dusty and ill-fitting gown, Meg with her arms draped around a filthy Blossom, Cassandra casually scratching Brutus's nose, and Finn and Jilly both looking like they were about to do battle.

"What's really going on?" Princess Wilhelmina said. "My father isn't back from the hunting lodge yet and—" She locked eyes with Anthea. "Your mother is at the lodge, isn't she?"

Anthea saw no reason to lie. "Yes."

"I thought you were taking a few days to have a little reunion," the princess said in a strangely flat voice.

"No," Anthea said.

"The horses needed her more," Finn said at the same time. "Her mother understands."

"I'm sure she does," Princess Wilhelmina said darkly. She looked over at Meg. "You're going to ruin that dress. But it doesn't fit you well anyway." She stalked out.

No one said anything until long after she was gone.

"That was odd, right?" Jilly said finally.

"Not really," Anthea said.

Everyone looked at her.

"How would you behave, if you walked into a room full of people who were all lying to you?"

Jilly made a face, nodding. "That's true. You know what else is true?"

"What?" Meg asked, gently taking a sponge to Blossom's back while the mare sighed with pleasure.

"Princess Wilhelmina absolutely, positively knows Anthea's mother. And she does not like her at all."

"That makes two of us," Anthea whispered to Florian as she ducked out of his stall to take care of Campanula.

"Oh, sweetheart," Aunt Cassandra said, coming to help her. "Don't worry about it! *No one* likes your mother."

DINNER

ROSE ACADEMY TRAINING SOUGHT to prepare young girls for every contingency. Along with literature, languages, mathematics, and the sciences, they were taught posture, deportment, dancing, music, conversation, table manners from various countries, and a host of other skills that would stand them in good stead if they were to be chosen as a companion to the queen. Of the many fine Rose Academies in Coronam, there were a handful that were legendary in their reputation for turning out the most accomplished young ladies, but one was lauded as the best of the best: Miss Miniver's Rose Academy, in Travertine.

When Anthea had been sent away from Travertine to live in the wild north with exiles and wild animals, she thought that she had at last found a situation where nothing learned at

Miss Miniver's could help her. But she was thankful for her dancing lessons, medals in posture and deportment, and ability to remain calm in chaotic situations whenever she sat on the back of a fractious horse. She also found herself studying math and science and literature, and having dinner with royalty, none of which she had expected, but all of which she had been trained to do.

But now, sitting at dinner surrounded by family and friends, looking at a plate of plain roast chicken and potatoes, Anthea knew. This was it. This was when her training finally failed her.

Because at no point during her years with Miss Miniver had that elegant lady taught what to do when sitting at a table with the emperor of Kronenhof, his two children, a hostage Kadiji prince, a hostage Coronami princess, the uncrowned king of a lost kingdom, an estranged aunt, uncle, and cousin, a long-lost aunt and her estranged daughter, and your mother, who had recently threatened to kill all your friends.

There was quite simply no precedent for this. No one had ever been put in such a position before. Even the redoubtable Miss Miniver would take to her bed with the vapors in such a situation.

Anthea cleared her throat, quietly.

"If you fake sick and leave, I'll never forgive you," Jilly whispered without moving her lips.

"I need to," Anthea whispered back, ducking her head to eat a bite of food.

It was delicious. It went down her throat like sawdust. She might be sick.

There was a rising tide of panic in her breast. Anthea honestly did not think she could continue to sit there pretending everything was fine. Everyone was watching her, waiting to see what she would do as Genevia and the emperor chatted about how long it would take to tame the wild Kronenhofer horses.

"I thought most Kronenhofer did not think the ghosts of the forest were real," Prince Adil said.

"The peasants have all manner of superstitions about them," Prince Fritz said. "But anyone who has been out in the forests hunting has seen them at least once."

"And no one has tried to tame them before now?" Finn looked skeptical. "I find that hard to believe."

"I don't recall them being so close to the palace before," Princess Wilhelmina said. "But we did have an especially hard winter, and—"

"The sauce on these potatoes is exceedingly delicious," Aunt Deirdre said. "I must confess that I have never given a great deal of thought to Kronenhofer cuisine, but everything has been scrumptious."

"Mother, stop changing the subject," Belinda Rose said, rolling her eyes. She turned to Prince Fritz, sitting beside her. "Do you ride horses, Your Highness?"

Jilly kicked Anthea under the table as Finn turned to make a face at her. Was Belinda Rose . . . flirting? With Prince Fritz? And so obviously that even Finn had noticed? Anthea wondered if she was delirious.

On Anthea's other side, Prince Adil lightly tapped her hand. He smiled when she looked at him, and said in a low voice, "I am so glad that all your charges are safely back in your care." He flicked his eyes, a lot more subtly than Belinda Rose ever could, toward Meg.

"All of them but Marius," Anthea said in an equally low voice, once she was sure that Deirdre was still discussing potatoes and that Fritz had embarked on a story about hunting. "Marius has run off with the ghosts," she whispered.

"Why?"

Anthea shrugged, pretending that she didn't know why.

She knew. Of course Marius had gone once they were close to getting Constantine back. Why wouldn't he choose to go off with some shy mares, to a place with no horrible herd stallion to lash out at him, where he wasn't constantly reminded that he wasn't good enough?

"So gloomy, Anthea," Genevia said from the end of the table.

She was seated at the foot, with the emperor at the head, a positioning not lost on Anthea. Princess Wilhelmina had always been the hostess at the schloss, but when they had assembled in the dining room tonight, it was Genevia who greeted everyone, and Genevia who ordered the footmen to show them all to their seats. Meg was at the emperor's right hand, which made sense, but Wilhelmina was along the side of the table, mixed in with the other guests like Anthea, Cassandra, Finn, and Jilly. Uncle Daniel was on the emperor's left hand, and he was openly plying Meg with questions about where she had been and what news, if any, she had from her family.

To Anthea's great relief, Meg remained as cool and proper as Anthea had ever seen her. She was simultaneously paying attention to the talk of fashions and potatoes, eating her meal with impeccable manners, and answering Uncle Daniel's questions in a bored manner that made him seem incredibly gauche for asking.

Anthea threw her shoulders back. If Meg could do it, so could she.

"I'm so sorry," Anthea said. "I hope I'm not spoiling anyone's dinner with my cloudy mood." She managed a smile. "I'm just terribly worried about the horses. The ones that had . . . wandered off. Heaven only knows where the poor things have been! We're very lucky that they didn't injure themselves permanently, running wild in a strange country!"

"Remember last year," Jilly put in. "Those farmers who saw Florian didn't know what a horse was, and tried to shoot him!" She clucked her tongue. "Just awful!"

"Someone shot your horse?" Princess Wilhelmina looked concerned. "Was the villain captured?"

"No," Anthea said. "I was too busy—"

"Being shot!" Jilly said dramatically. "They missed Florian, but they shot Anthea! And hurt Bluebell! And that was after Leonidas had been caught in a snare."

"You've been shot?" Belinda Rose looked torn between being impressed and horrified.

"Jillian, we are *eating*," Aunt Cassandra said.

"She was barely hurt," Genevia said dismissively. "And the horses only had a few scratches. I saw them immediately after."

Everyone turned to look at Anthea's mother. She seemed to realize a moment too late that she had just made a very large mistake.

"I thought you had not seen your daughter since she was a baby," Emperor Wilhelm said.

"I was under the same impression," Uncle Daniel said. "It would have been useful to know, while the rest of us were shouldering the burden of caring for your child, that you were flitting about nearby!"

"Did you just call Thea a burden?" Jilly said dangerously.

"I—I may have run afoul of her—I mean, of people trying to harm her and her horses! Well, last year or so," Genevia said, flustered. "But soon the Dag broke out, and there was such chaos and—"

"Afoul?" Jilly said, her face livid.

"It was surely some months between Thea's first stay with

us at Bell Hyde and the Dag breaking out?" Meg said, artless confusion on her face.

Anthea felt a surge of warmth toward her friends. She was also very amused that it appeared even her mother's training had failed. The emperor and Uncle Daniel were exchanging meaningful looks. And glares.

"The important thing," Finn said loudly, "is that there was no permanent harm done. Florian never would have allowed Thea to be seriously injured."

"But look at her scar!" Belinda Rose sounded almost gleeful.

"I think it's distinctive," Finn said.

Anthea wasn't sure if that was a good thing or a bad thing.

"It's piratical," Prince Fritz said. "I've always wanted a roguish scar!"

Jilly knocked her knee against Anthea's, and when Anthea glanced at her, Jilly waggled her own, unscarred, eyebrows. Anthea had never wanted to be a pirate, but in Prince Fritz's mind it was a compliment, so she smiled and accepted it as such.

"Of course I didn't want my daughter *scarred*," Genevia said.

"You didn't want your daughter at all," Uncle Daniel snarled.

The table sat in an uncomfortable silence before Prince Adil suddenly announced, "I have two theories about the ghosts in the forest."

Everyone looked at him in surprise. Anthea shot him a relieved smile, which he answered.

"And what would *you* know about Kronenhofer legends?" Wilhelm laughed.

A ripple of anger passed over Adil's face. Anthea could see him willing himself not to retort. But instead the prince replied very mildly, which is probably how he had managed to survive so long in this place.

"I spend a great deal of time reading," Prince Adil said. "You have a very fine library here. A great many scholars visit, because of its extensive collection of books on Kronenhofer history."

Miss Miniver herself would have been proud of his even tone and utterly smooth expression.

"A long time ago there was a great deal of easy trade between Kronenhof and Leana," Adil continued. "Whether the horses were all originally from Leana and brought here as part of a trading deal, or whether there was a great deal of trade because Kronenhof also had horses, no one is quite sure."

"Do the people of Kronenhof have the Way?" Jilly asked eagerly.

"My theory is that they do, or at least some of them do. Or did," Prince Adil said. "I believe that horses were brought from Leana, by people who had the Way. But then they got loose or were let go."

"Why?" Anthea asked. "How could they . . . ?"

She found she had a lump in her throat. How could anyone who had the Way just give up their horse? It was too horrible to even think about!

"Because of the stones," Prince Adil said. He was leaning over the table, clearly excited to have an audience for his findings. "The stones here give off some sort of . . . well, I don't know what to call it. An odor? An aura? Something that blocks the Way. You've noticed this, I'm sure," he said to Anthea and her companions, but didn't wait for an answer. He was too deep into his theory to notice their frozen expressions. "I believe that when Leanan riders came here and found that the Way had stopped working, they let their horses loose and the animals became feral."

"There's a magic rock that prevents this 'Way' from working?" Emperor Wilhelm looked skeptical. "A convenient sort of excuse."

"Excuse for what?" Finn asked.

"For bad behavior," he said.

Anthea could not help herself. "Then why did you have one of the standing stones, carved from this very rock, brought all the way from northern Coronam to your hunting lodge?" She made her voice as innocent as possible. "Your Imperial Highness," she added after a beat.

The twinkle in Meg's eyes was matched only by that in Adil's.

"What do you mean? That cannot be the same stone," Emperor Wilhelm said with every appearance of confusion. "Your mother merely wanted something to remind her of her home."

"And you believe—" Jilly began, but she winced and stopped short as someone, either her mother or possibly Finn, kicked her ankle.

"I have worked extensively with the Crown over the past year," Uncle Daniel said. "King Gareth was initially pleased that this Way might be a useful method of carrying messages to remote villages, or for transmitting . . . sensitive information."

"You mean spying," Jilly said. "The word you want is 'spying.'"

No one kicked her this time. Uncle Daniel looked over her head and simply declined to answer.

"But," he continued, "once the Crown actually commissioned the horses and riders to do this work . . . suddenly the Way wasn't working. It was too far. The weather wasn't right." His voice was mocking.

"I don't recall complaining about the weather," Finn said, his voice icy. "Not even when the cowardly king had us nearly working our men and horses to death in the cold and wet."

Deirdre gasped theatrically. Belinda Rose put her hands over her ears. Princess Wilhelmina looked away in polite shock. Meg went pale.

"How dare you say such a thing about the Crown!" Daniel rose from his seat. "This is treason!"

"In order for it to be treason," Finn said, "Gareth will have to decide if I am his vassal or his brother king."

"Which do you want to be?" Emperor Wilhelm was quick to ask.

Anthea heard Aunt Cassandra take in a slow breath and then let it out. Everyone looked at Finn, who locked eyes with the emperor and didn't waver.

"According to yourself, sir, I am a crown prince," Finn answered. "The uncrowned ruler of the nation of Leana."

"It's quite true," Genevia said. "His Imperial Majesty has shown you all such courtesy while you have been here. As visiting dignitaries, if you want to be taken seriously, you should reciprocate in some way."

Even though her words were supposed to be for Finn, her eyes were on Anthea. They had been on Anthea throughout dinner, when they were not giving meaningful looks to the emperor. Anthea felt as though her mother's gaze weighed twenty pounds.

"We would be very pleased to try and capture some of the local horses and find out if they do, indeed, communicate the same way that ours do. We could send people to help train them," Finn said at last.

"Send people?" Wilhelmina sounded upset. "Aren't you staying yourself?"

"I promised my cousin Josephine that I\would escort Meg home," Finn said.

"And, although I've been here such a short time, I would like to return home soon," Meg said.

"Is Kronenhofer hospitality so distasteful to you?" Genevia asked.

Anthea met Jilly's gaze and raised her eyebrows.

"It has been wonderful," Meg said. "But I have been away far too long, and I feel guilty about not telling anyone where I was going. I need to beg forgiveness for worrying my father and mother so!"

Whoever Meg's governess was, Anthea thought, the woman must be the consummate Rose Maiden. Jilly subtly tilted her glass at Meg in a sly toast, and the emperor's eyes narrowed. But Deirdre and Daniel looked oblivious, nodding approval at Meg's remorse.

"And what if these rocks keep your people from training our horses . . . Lord Finn?" Wilhelm said. "What if it isn't magic rocks, but that our horses are not the same? They do not look the same. They are less impressive, physically."

"We won't know until we try," Finn said. "I have several theories about the way they look. There's the rocky ground to consider, the lack of open space to run, not to mention breeding—"

"But before you go, Princess Margaret, you must allow us to celebrate!" Wilhelmina interjected, dismissing the talk of horses.

"Yes, of course," the emperor agreed. "The ball tomorrow night, and I think a parade would not be out of order? I'm sure that my people would love to see a foreign princess of such beauty mounted on a tame horse! The stuff of legends!"

Meg smiled with relief. "I would be greatly honored!" She raised her glass of lemonade to toast the emperor.

"It will be an excellent opportunity for me to introduce the people to my horse as well," Wilhelm went on.

Anthea felt all the color bleed from her face. She put her glass down, not having the strength to hold it up.

"I'm afraid that's not enough time to tame one of the ghosts," Finn said. "We're still trying to find them. And I promised to escort Meg personally, to make sure she doesn't run off again." He managed to make it sound like a joke.

"Oh, that's not a problem," Genevia said. "In fact, we assumed you would leave with Princess Margaret.

"I'll just keep my daughter here to help with the horses. After all, who better to teach His Imperial Majesty to ride Florian, than Florian's former rider?"

BEGIN THE COUNT AGAIN

"IT'S QUITE SIMPLE," JILLY said. "You leave now, with Florian and Bluebell, we meet you at the ship.

"We could disguise you first. Cut your hair, dress you up..."

She pursed her lips, already plotting how best to conceal Anthea. They were in Anthea's room, after dinner, and Anthea was still numb. Added to that was a feeling of claustrophobia. Her mother had her trapped; as much as she was tempted by Jilly's escape plan, Anthea knew she wouldn't use it. Too much was at stake.

"Don't cut it!" Finn said. He reached out like he was going to touch Anthea's long tail of hair.

Jilly blinked at him. "Excuse me?"

"I mean, there's no way to hide the horses," Finn said, and

hastily withdrew his hand. "It's not like we can dress them up in dog costumes! So there's no need to do . . . to do anything so drastic to Anthea!"

"What will the emperor do if you leave?" Jilly asked. "If you just get on the ship with us? He won't actually start a war—" She stopped.

They all knew that the emperor would. He, and Genevia, had indeed attempted to—twice, in fact.

Anthea let them think it was war she was worried about. It was better than telling them her real fear: that her mother would kill them.

"I can stay longer," Meg said anxiously. "Maybe that would give you time to train the ghosts?"

"It's a nice thought, dear, but we need to get you home as soon as possible," Cassandra said. "I've already sent word to your mother and father. Hopefully they'll get the letter in time . . ."

Nobody needed her to finish that sentence. They all knew that Gareth would not order his own army to stand down until he saw Meg in person.

Beloved?

Anthea lurched to her feet.

What is it, my darling?

They are here.

Through the Way Anthea could smell the dead roses of her mother's perfume. All Rose Maidens and Matrons wore it; the Crown's personal perfumer specially made it for them. But Genevia seemed to have added something to it that made it stronger, more cloying ... faintly toxic, when passing through a horse's nose.

Anthea took off running. She heard the others shouting behind her but didn't stop. By the time she reached the endless stretch of lawn that led to the stable, Finn had caught up to her.

"They haven't touched them," Finn panted. "Con won't let them."

But Anthea didn't slow down. And when she found the stable doors blocked by the emperor's guards, she raised her scarred eyebrow and they leaped aside for her. Anthea wondered fleetingly what her expression looked like.

"What are you doing?"

That was what she cared about. She cared about Emperor Wilhelm standing in front of the stall that Florian and Leonidas shared, the two stallions backed into the far corner so that he couldn't touch them.

Now that her heart wasn't pounding so loudly in her ears, she could hear Constantine neighing in the way that usually prefaced his herd stallion scream. He was pawing at the straw and looked ready to burst right through the wooden rail that served as a gate.

Before Anthea could repeat the question, Genevia smiled.

"Oh, good, you're here," she said.

She was standing beside Wilhelm. With them were Fritz and Uncle Daniel. Anthea was almost relieved to see that neither Adil nor Wilhelmina was there.

Finn put a hand on Anthea's elbow and escorted her into the middle of the stable. He put his free hand on Constantine's neck. Jilly ran in and stopped herself from flying headfirst into Uncle Daniel by wrapping an arm around Anthea's waist.

"We know that you sneak around, spying on the horses when we aren't here," Anthea said to Wilhelm. "It's not going to make Florian forget me and bond to you."

"That's not why I do it," he said, laughing.

Uncle Daniel, who had been swelling with indignation at Anthea's belligerence, checked abruptly. Anthea could almost hear the air leaking out of him like a punctured balloon, but it was almost exactly how she felt as well.

"Then why?" Finn said. His indignation was very much intact.

"Because I *can*," Emperor Wilhelm said. "I can come here anytime, day or night. This is my shed, in my garden, in my schloss, in my country. My empire!" His gray eyes locked with Anthea's. "And if I say you will give me your horse, *you will give me your horse*."

"Or what?" Jilly said.

"Or you die," the emperor said.

Jilly actually burst out laughing. It was such a completely ridiculous statement that Anthea would have joined her, had she not already been threatened with this very thing by her mother. She knew Wilhelm was good to his word. He was like a snake mesmerizing a mouse so that it wouldn't struggle while being eaten.

"Is this how you treat your fellow royals?" Finn said.

Emperor Wilhelm's voice was silky, his eyes still on Anthea. "Fellow royal? Do you really think that anyone would notice if you went missing?"

"My father—" Jilly began.

"I meant anyone of importance," Wilhelm said.

Jilly gasped in outrage, and Buttercup and Caesar pawed at the ground.

"If King Gareth ever noticed, he would probably send me a gift to thank me for getting rid of the pebble in his shoe. For that is all you are: a pebble. The tiniest little inconvenience."

"If you kill me, or any of us, you will find out how terrible the retribution of our horses and the rest of the riders can be," Finn said.

"More terrible than having my great, armored schutzerlei roll over your villages?" Emperor Wilhelm asked.

"We destroyed them," Finn countered. "Or had you forgotten? I realize it has been two whole days."

Emperor Wilhelm laughed, loud and long and joyously. Genevia joined in with a warm chuckle. Anthea let Jilly squeeze her waist tighter, but she moved closer to Finn, clamping his hand against her side. He was shaking.

"Do you think that was all we had? Those two little machines?" He shook his head. "Those were my *personal* machines, the ones that I sometimes let Madame Genevia use." His eyes hardened and the merriment left his face. "Now imagine an entire army of those, but larger. Faster."

"Then why are you trying to take my horses?" Anthea cried out.

Emperor Wilhelm smiled. "Because I can," he said. "Power isn't always about brute force, little girl. I can tear down walls with the schutzerlei *and* send spies to kidnap a young prince from under his father's very nose. Why should I not also have the wonderful horses that can speak across the miles with their riders? The schutzerlei are impressive, but the horses are far more elegant.

"More elegant, and more intelligent, than our forest ghosts. You will help us get rid of the stones, you will teach your horse to speak to me, and you will smile while you do it.

"I am the emperor of Kronenhof. And I will have them all."

Anthea realized that she was also shaking, but from rage, not fear. She realized, too, that Finn was leaning against her not because he was afraid of the emperor, but because he was afraid of lashing out at Wilhelm.

Uncle Daniel cleared his throat. "Well, I think perhaps—" he began.

"Stop talking," Anthea said in a low voice.

Genevia opened her mouth, but Anthea shook her head, hard.

"And you," she said. "I don't want to hear a word from any of you."

"Anthea," Genevia said with a strong note of warning in her voice.

"Your Imperial Highness," Uncle Daniel said. "I have some things I must speak to you about in private." But his eyes were on Anthea, and his face was uneasy.

Anthea did not care. She took a step forward, and Finn and Jilly relaxed their grip on her just enough so that she could walk to Florian's stall. The adults parted and edged around them, going out of the stable. Anthea could dimly hear her uncle start to say something in a low voice, but she didn't bother to try and listen.

Jilly kissed Anthea's head before she let go and went to Buttercup. But Finn kept his arm around Anthea until she reached Florian. He squeezed her waist gently before letting go. She almost thought he was going to kiss her as well, but he turned suddenly and went to Constantine.

Anthea held out her arms. Both her stallions came forward and hung their heads over each of her shoulders. She hugged their necks.

My beautiful brave boys, Anthea said. *I am so sorry.*

It is not your fault, Our Anthea, Leonidas said.

He raised his head and lipped at her hair, then he backed

away and went to stand at the divider between his stall and Bluebell's. The mare put her head over, and Anthea could tell that the horses were conferring.

Anthea buried her face in Florian's mane.

Beloved.

My love, my love.

I will not forsake you.

You should! See what I have done! You are hurt, and we are trapped here, so far from home!

Nothing matters except that we are together.

Is that enough? What if we never see our home again?

Beloved, we will go home. I will take you home.

Hot tears slipped from Anthea's eyes into Florian's thick black mane. She held him tightly and just let the sobs overtake her.

Constantine, Florian, and Bluebell

Florian, while you are outside this poor excuse of a stable, search for Marius.

I will, Herd Stallion.

We must go as soon as possible, but we cannot leave Marius behind. Although the temptation is strong. He failed the Now King by being weak, and now he has failed through cowardice!

He was trying to draw out the mares of this place, who have not lived among men. They are too frightened to speak to the Now King or even my own Beloved!

Perhaps, or perhaps he has abandoned our herd!

I will look for him, but I will not force him to come back. Not if you are going to punish him.

You dare defy me? You dare decree who I can and cannot punish?

You were not there; you did not try to outrace the terrible machines! You do not know of Marius's strength in making this journey. You did not see him try to speak with the strange mares, to get them to trust the Now King and join our herd!

This is true. But it is also true that he is gone now, and has not tried to return without the mares.

Perhaps this awful stone has muddled his mind.

You are not muddled. I am not muddled. Leonidas and Brutus are not muddled! The mares—

Do not speak for us, Herd Stallion! Do not presume! We do not blame Marius for going elsewhere. We are none of us fond of these stones or of being under the eye of That Bearded King.

Forgive me, gentle mare Bluebell. I—

Though I would not presume to think that I am as closely bonded to Our Dear Anthea as Florian, it is greatly distressing not to feel her presence even when she is only a quick trot across the lawns. Greatly distressing, too, to have one with the Way come and stare, but refuse to speak!

Who? That Bearded King?

No. As you yourself know, Herd Stallion, he does not have the Way. Is that not so, Florian?

I can find no spark of it . . . Bluebell.

I speak of the mother of Our Dear Anthea, that Woman Who Smells of Dead Roses. She has the Way but will not use it. It makes me itch as much as the stones.

I do not think she has been near enough to me for me to discover this. You are clever to sense it, Bluebell.

I did think it likely, when she spoke to me when I was taken at the village and also on the crossing over the water. It was as though she wished to change my mood but not speak with me! Disgusting.

Something is very wrong with her, and now she has made Beloved Anthea grieve. This cannot be. I will watch for Marius today, and I hope that being close to my Beloved and away from the stones in this forest will help me fix our problem.

Good Florian, turn your mind only to Our Dear Anthea and finding a way for us all to leave. I will keep watch for Marius and the wild mares.

Thank you . . . good Bluebell. I will do this.

Yes. These are your tasks.

Yes, Herd Stallion.

Yes, Herd Stallion.

23

A SUBTLE TRAP

"THERE IS NO PART of this that I like," Finn announced.

"Oh, really?" Jilly drawled. "I, for one, *love* this. I love everything from the extremely itchy lace of this blouse to the exposed feeling of riding Caesar down a street full of strangers who might all be carrying guns."

"They won't have guns at a parade," Meg said. Her brow clouded. "Will they?"

"No! Why would they?" Aunt Cassandra assured her.

"Why do the Kronenhofer do anything?" Finn grumbled.

Anthea used the huge gilt-framed mirror on the wall of Aunt Cassandra's room to adjust her coat. She was also wearing a lace blouse underneath, and fitted riding trousers, like Jilly and Meg.

Meg wore a velvet jacket, and Jilly had hand-embroidered

her own coat with roses and horses along the hem and sleeves. Anthea's beloved gray army coat was too big and too plain . . . and she loved it. It was her armor, and she needed it today more than ever. She adjusted it across her shoulders one more time, and made sure that the charms pinned to the lapels—a rose, a horseshoe, and an emerald brooch Aunt Cassandra had given her—were secure.

Anthea caught her aunt's eye in the mirror and gave a weak smile in response to Aunt Cassandra's approving nod. Jilly and Finn had asked twice that morning if she was all right, but Aunt Cassandra sensed that she wasn't, and had been deflecting the others' chatter and concerns from Anthea.

"It's time to begin this idiocy," Finn said.

As they went down to the stables, Aunt Cassandra walking with her arm linked in Meg's, Jilly ventured to ask why Finn was in a bad mood.

"Isn't this what we've always wanted? *King Finn!*"

"My mother's going to be so pleased," Meg said. "From the letters you've shown me, she's been working hard on this very thing back home, too!"

"Exactly," Finn said. "Back home. Where it's still not official. Being recognized as a king in Kronenhof, when my kingdom is across an ocean is . . . strange? Idiotic?"

"Actually," Aunt Cassandra said, "it's still very good for you, and for Leana." She shrugged. "Anytime a foreign ruler recognizes another foreign ruler, it gives them an added measure of legitimacy. Frankly, I've been worried that only Gareth would recognize your claim."

"Why worried?" Anthea asked, finally feeling a spark of interest penetrate the fog that enshrouded her.

"Well," Aunt Cassandra said, "I think, and Andrew agrees with me, that if only Gareth stands behind you it merely feels patronizing. Like a courtesy title handed out as reward for services to the Crown. There's no clearly defined boundaries to Leana anymore, and—"

"Isn't the Wall good enough?" Finn asked with asperity.

"Not when Upper Stonesraugh is miles to the south of it," Aunt Cassandra retorted. "No, things need to be made more concrete, and they need to be made more . . . international, lest this merely be seen as a Coronami matter."

"Being recognized by Kronenhof will make my father more amenable to calling you a king," Meg told Finn. "I mean, not really *amenable*." She gave a little laugh. "But if his biggest rival says you are a king, he'll have to say it, too, just so that he doesn't get left behind."

"My father, too, supports you," said Prince Adil, meeting them at the door of the stables. "I wrote to him as soon as I met you, intrigued by your story." He held up a letter. "I have just received this. Based on what I have said, and my research about horses and the lost kingdom of Leana, he has no doubt that you are its rightful king. Kadij recognizes your claim, Your Majesty."

"Thank you," Finn said, sounding a little choked up.

Prince Adil bowed to Finn, and Finn bowed back, Aunt Cassandra throwing out a hand to stop him from bowing too deeply. She looked very pleased, and Anthea felt a wild stirring of hope in her own breast.

Perhaps she could write to Adil's father and tell him of her plight? He would surely be sympathetic to another young person being held hostage by the Kronenhofer empire! But if he were too afraid to move on behalf of his own son, would he take the risk for someone he didn't know? Anthea felt her hope dissipate, though not entirely. She clung to some of it, a shred. She had to, because now she had to face Florian.

Jilly suddenly latched onto something her mother had just said. "Did you say that Da agreed with you?" she asked, suspicious. "When did he say that?"

"I do correspond with your father, Jilly," Cassandra said airily.

"Since when? And . . . are you *blushing*?"

Anthea stepped into the welcome warmth and straw-smell of the stable.

Hello, my darling! She managed to sound cheerful. *How are you this morning?*

I am well, Beloved. Are you . . . are you well?

Of course I am well! I am only a little homesick, she lied.

Well, partially lied. As soon as the word "homesick" crossed her mind she felt a surge of longing for the Last Farm that almost took her breath away. To sleep in her own bed! And ride Florian and Bluebell around the familiar green paddocks!

And now we must go on parade?

That's right! We will go down the streets of the city, to the government buildings, and they will bow to the Now King, and they will greet the New Meg, and take photographs to show to Josephine, Beloved of Holly.

But why?

To show that she is safe.

But they know she is not.

She is now. It is complicated. And stupid.

I do not think she is safe.

Anthea didn't think any of them were safe. But all they could do was try to stay as safe as possible, by playing Genevia's latest game. Although it was really only Anthea who had to play, in order to keep the others safe. And she couldn't even tell them for fear that they would try something foolish.

But there was no way to defeat Genevia. None that Anthea could see.

"Wait," Jilly said as they started to saddle the horses. "What are you doing?"

Anthea was putting one of Finn's spare saddles on Florian. It was wider than Anthea's and barely any higher in the back than the front, so it would accommodate Emperor Wilhelm's larger bottom. Anthea would need to lengthen the stirrups, which is what her mind was busy with when she realized what Jilly had asked.

"Why don't you use your good saddle?" Jilly asked.

"I'm going to ride Bluebell," Anthea said quietly.

"Then who is riding Florian?" Finn asked with an edge to his voice.

Nobody talked for a minute, and only Anthea moved. She kept putting on the tack, her hands moving automatically. Florian shifted uneasily, throwing his head up and making it hard for her to put the bridle on him.

"Hush, my love," Anthea murmured.

"You're going to let the emperor ride him?" Jilly said in a horrified whisper, as though Anthea's words to Florian had been an answer.

"You know that I have to," Anthea whispered.

Jilly reached over and squeezed Anthea's shoulder. "I'm sorry," she murmured.

"It's going to be all right," Finn said.

He was in the stall with Anthea, saddling Leonidas. He reached out, and then awkwardly brushed his hand against her face and shoulder.

"The sooner we get out of here, the better," Meg said.

She was going to ride Juniper since Blossom was still healing, and this made Blossom anxious. Meg finally had to let Blossom stand close enough to be reassured as the princess tacked up Juniper.

The one good thing to come of pretending that Genevia had not abducted either princess or horses was that their saddles had appeared in the stable.

"We should have better saddle blankets made," Jilly said. "Something with the Horse Maiden symbol on it for us." She indicated herself, Anthea, and Meg. "And something with the Leanan flag for Finn and the rest of the riders."

"What does the Leanan flag look like?" Meg asked.

"I don't think there ever was one," Finn admitted. "The kings and the major families, like the MacRennies and the mag-Tarans, had personal symbols. Braided patterns shaped like horseshoes that they used to mark their horses and property."

He pulled out the charm he wore under his shirt. It was a horseshoe, but this one wasn't smooth like the ones the girls wore. Instead it was etched with angular shapes that almost—but not quite—made a pattern. Anthea found that her eyes wanted to follow it in a continuous line that wasn't there.

"Da has something like that," Jilly said, admiring. "He wears it under his clothes, too."

"It's the ancient Leanan language, and for a long time it was illegal, much like the horseshoe itself," Finn said, tucking it away.

Meg shook her head. "I don't understand how my family can pretend they were only getting rid of horses because of disease! How do you make *jewelry* illegal, and claim it's because of disease?"

"Men do a lot of strange things," Jilly said knowingly, and Meg nodded.

They finished saddling up the horses and emerged from the stable to find the emperor waiting for them. Anthea felt like a black cloud had rolled over her again. Genevia was standing at his side, of course, wearing a crisp scarlet suit the exact color of the Kronenhofer flag and a magnificent hat topped with ostrich feathers. There was not a single rose to be seen on her person, but Anthea could smell her perfume from several paces away.

"Are you going to ride?" Jilly asked.

"No, I had my fill of that years ago," Genevia said.

No mare would let her *on their back*, Bluebell said.

Now? Or then? Anthea asked. She had an image of her mother being bucked across a paddock at the Last Farm, and a smile tweaked her mouth.

Now, Bluebell said. *She never came near us before.*

Were you alive? Do you remember her?

It occurred to Anthea that she didn't know how old Bluebell was. She had never asked if the mare had known her father, let alone her mother. It wasn't just that Anthea's bond with Florian was stronger—none of the mares were very talkative, even with their riders.

I was not alive then, but my mother remembers her, Bluebell said. *I am eight*, Bluebell added. *My mother's name is Posey. My father's name does not matter. I wish to have a foal when we return home. It is time.*

Oh. Oh! All right, Anthea said.

She hunched her shoulders in guilt. They wouldn't be returning home anytime soon.

"It's very rude to talk about people behind their backs," Genevia said archly, watching Anthea's face.

"Fine," Anthea said. She looked Emperor Wilhelm dead in the eye. "None of the horses want to carry you, but Florian will because I told him he must. Sit up straight in the saddle and don't make any sudden moves."

If he falls off, Beloved, I don't care if he gets back on.

Frankly, my darling, neither do I.

24

THE FIRST PARADE

"I'VE SEEN A SACK of potatoes look better on horseback," Jilly said out of the side of her mouth.

"When did you see a sack of potatoes on horseback?" Anthea said.

The day was cool, but Anthea could feel beads of sweat sparkling at her hairline. Florian was on edge—all the horses were. Anthea was keeping up a steady stream of reassurance to him, Bluebell, and Leonidas, who, although he was proud to carry the Now King, was showing even more nerves than the other horses.

Anthea wanted to ride forward and stroke Leonidas's neck, perhaps tug Florian's forelock. But that was impossible in this tight formation. Emperor Wilhelm, on Florian, was at the front of the parade, gripping the reins and staring straight ahead.

Anthea was more than a little pleased to see how terrified he was of falling off, though it was rather insulting as well. Florian had once carried her unconscious on his back. He had the smoothest gait of any horse she had ever ridden, and a strong wide back that Uncle Andrew joked must be like riding on a sofa. But to the emperor of Kronenhof it was akin to sitting astride a loaded cannon, or so Jilly had joked. Anthea prayed that the experience would convince Emperor Wilhelm that he did not want a horse, and he would consequently let them go.

After him, side by side, came the "royal cousins" Meg and Finn. They both smiled, turning their heads to look at the crowd, holding their reins loosely in one hand so that they could wave with the other. After them came Anthea and Jilly, who was blowing kisses at the children. Anthea was trying not to look strained as she kept three horses from bolting.

It helped that people waved back. Children stood as close as they dared and tossed flowers in front of the horses. Some of them waved tiny Kronenhofer and Coronami flags. Anthea could tell that some of the children wanted to run out and touch the horses, but their parents held them back. The parents did not appear half as enamored as the children did. Anthea supposed that growing up with stories of the "ghosts of the forest" had a great deal to do with it.

Behind the horses came the cars from the palace, their leather tops folded back so that those riding inside could do their share of waving. Princess Wilhelmina probably found driving slowly just as stressful as Anthea found keeping the horses to a walk. Aunt Cassandra was sitting beside her mother, which gave Anthea comfort—a force for good ready to counteract any vileness her mother might spew.

Any additional vileness, anyway. Her mother had already done so much harm that it would be impossible to truly repair it. There was still the matter of convincing King Gareth not to go to war with Kronenhof, and to recognize Finn as a brother king. And the equally important matter of acknowledging loudly and publicly that the horses had nothing to do with either the Dag or any other badness that the Crown had laid at their hooves.

It was going to be a long, grim fight. And Anthea wouldn't be there to help.

Yes, you will, Bluebell said.

I don't think you're supposed to read my every thought, she retorted.

Then stop thinking so loudly! You're making the stallions nervous!

I am not, Anthea protested weakly.

She probably was.

The broad street opened up into a great circular drive that looped around a fountain featuring a stern goddess pouring water from a massive urn. And on the other side of the fountain was the mighty curved behemoth that housed the everyday workings of the empire.

A broad scarlet carpet had been laid right down the steps to the pavement, and now they circled the fountain to stop just at its edge. Anthea was tempted to order Florian to walk right up the carpeted steps and into the *Palast Kanzlerei*. Instead she called a silent halt to all the horses at the edge and they stopped neatly in a line, with the emperor nearest the steps.

He slumped with relief, but only for a second. Then his back was straight as a board once more. They all sat on their horses in a row, stiff and silent, and waited.

The cars pulled past them and parked on the other side of the carpet. No one got out. They all sat and stared ahead through the windscreens at the horses. A line of ministers and ambassadors were waiting up on the top of the stairs, in front of the doors. They didn't move, either.

There was a man with a camera positioned a little to one side. He took a picture just as Anthea looked his way, and the flash blinded her temporarily. Bluebell shifted from foot to foot, and Anthea blindly stroked her mane.

Caesar says that She Who Is Jilly says, How long do we have to sit here? And that the Bearded Emperor doesn't know how to dismount, Bluebell reported. *I don't like Caesar talking to me*, she added sulkily.

Tell Caesar to tell Jilly that no one can dismount or get out of the motorcars until the emperor does, Anthea said. *And I'm sorry Caesar bothers you, but we all have to work together.*

He should not have addressed me first, Bluebell huffed.

This isn't a time for niceties, Anthea snapped before she turned to Florian.

Florian, my darling? Is there any way you can get the emperor off your back without tossing him on the ground?

I will not kneel for him. Florian's voice was terse.

It struck Anthea, horribly, like an actual physical blow. Florian *could* kneel and allow the emperor to simply step off. But this was something horses did with their most beloved riders only.

Finn turned his head and looked at Anthea. She saw it in his eyes, too.

Smoothly, casually, Finn dismounted. Then he grabbed Florian's reins and sketched a salute to the emperor, as though this had been the plan all along.

He must have whispered some instructions to Wilhelm, because the emperor let go of the reins and grabbed the front of the saddle. Slowly, awkwardly, Wilhelm got his right leg out of the stirrup and swung it over Florian's back. Anthea sent reassuring thoughts to Florian, bidding him to be still, but he didn't answer. Though his ears flicked forward and he didn't move a muscle, despite the ungainly way the emperor half fell off his back.

Once Wilhelm was on his own two feet, Meg gracefully dismounted, followed by Jilly, and then Anthea. The others got out of the motorcars, and they all stepped onto the red carpet.

"Please let me stay with the horses," Jilly muttered.

"We probably both should," Anthea said.

"Jilly, stay with the horses," Cassandra said. "Anthea, we need you inside."

They didn't have far to go. Just up the carpeted stairs and into the magnificent rotunda at the center of the *palast*. The floor was of marble, black and white and inlaid in a herringbone pattern, but so carefully polished as to be seamless. Finn took Anthea's elbow when she slipped stepping off the carpet, but Anthea jerked free when she saw her mother watching and smiling.

A small table had been set up in the middle of the rotunda. There were electric lights all around the room, but a more grayish spring light filtered in from the high round windows set into the dome far above their heads. The table held a map and some papers and gold pens.

There were hands to shake: the rotunda was filled with ministers and ambassadors, counts and lords. The photographer had followed them in, and he kept running around, setting up his tripod, taking a picture that blinded anyone who happened to look his way, and then moving again. Anthea thought of the photographer who had taken photographs of the riders last year in Coronam, the one they had teased for also being named Arthur. She wondered if he had survived the Dag. He had been much less irritating than this Kronenhofer photographer.

Prince Adil appeared. Anthea had thought he was supposed to be in the parade, but he had not gotten into any of the cars. He made a little gesture like he wanted to speak to her, but she couldn't step away now; and where would they go? Into the massive, echoing parliamentary chambers?

Beloved, something is amiss, Florian reported.

Anthea jumped. After so many weeks of barely being able to hear her horses unless she was riding on them, she did not expect to hear Florian's voice so clearly when he was outside a building.

Caesar said to tell you that She Who Is Jilly says that there is no funny gray stone in the city, Bluebell reported.

Assuming that Prince Adil had wanted to tell her that, Anthea nodded back at him more meaningfully. She pointed to the marble floor, then nodded again.

Prince Adil just looked baffled. He tried to sidle closer to her, but Meg and Finn were blocking his path.

They were all standing in a semicircle around the little table. Clustered beyond it were various ministers and ambassadors, including Uncle Daniel. Emperor Wilhelm stood next to the table, surveying the group in front of him with great pleasure. It made Anthea's skin crawl.

"We welcome Princess Margaret of Coronam here to Kronenhof," Emperor Wilhelm intoned. "Coronam, our neighbor to the north, has always been our ally. It has grieved us to be at odds with them these past few months. The vicious attack on one of our ships in Coronami waters . . . well! I shall speak no more of it! Because today we make great strides toward a more permanent friendship!"

He turned and waved to Prince Fritz, who had driven the second motorcar and was lurking a little behind, looking uncomfortable in his formal uniform. The last time Anthea had seen him thus attired had been at the very first reception and ball they had attended. His usual devil-may-care smile was gone, too, and his hair was so neatly combed and pomaded that Anthea didn't think it could move.

Fritz came forward, swallowing, and reached out for Meg. Her blond eyebrows were knotted together, but she took his hand in an automatic gesture. Emperor Wilhelm nodded and snapped his fingers at the photographer, who took a picture of the two standing in the middle of the rotunda holding hands.

Anthea gasped. Her aunt Cassandra jabbed her in the side with an elbow, but Cassandra's eyes were shadowed. Anthea struggled to emulate her aunt's blank expression, but inside she was screaming.

Bluebell, ask Caesar to ask Jilly if the New Meg and the Prince Fritz are . . . if she knew that they . . .

What is it, Dear Anthea?

Tell Caesar to tell She Who Is Jilly that . . .

But Anthea stopped. Jilly would surely come storming in, demanding to know what was going on. And there was no way that Meg and Fritz had, what? Fallen in love? Two days after they met? Although judging from their faces and their stiff posture, neither of them had any idea that this was going to happen.

"Not official," Aunt Cassandra whispered without moving her mouth. "Can't be."

"Madness," Finn whispered.

His whisper was very quiet, but the emperor turned at once, making an imperious gesture for Finn to come forward. As soon as his father's attention had shifted, Fritz dropped Meg's hand. But he did escort her away from the table to stand in the semicircle, his head hanging.

Perhaps he had known his father's plan, but he clearly did not like it.

And now it was Finn's turn. Finn, tall and blond and frankly far more regal looking than Fritz, despite his lack of uniform and medals, strode over and stood in front of the table with the emperor.

After snapping his fingers at the photographer again, Wilhelm grasped Finn's hand and held it firmly, gazing deeply into Finn's eyes for an uncomfortably long time. As clearly as if her cousin were standing beside her, Anthea heard Jilly's voice in her head whispering, "Are they betrothed now, too?" and almost laughed aloud.

Once the emperor and Finn parted, Wilhelm went to the table and took up a piece of paper and a pen.

"I hereby recognize the sovereignty of Leana," Wilhelm

announced, scribbling. "And that Finn magTaran is the rightful king thereof. I hereby pledge to be an ally to Leana, and to Finn magTaran."

He signed the paper with a flourish, and then put the date underneath. A scarlet wafer of wax was placed at the bottom and Wilhelm pressed his signet ring into it with unnecessary force. A line formed, and half a dozen ministers came forward to sign in the space left beneath the imperial seal.

Anthea's uncle Daniel hovered at the edge. Anthea watched as Genevia glided over to him and whispered in his ear. She saw, for the first time, the family resemblance: their straight noses and the arch of their eyebrows were clearly from the father they shared.

Daniel shook his head, just slightly. Genevia nudged his elbow, tilting her head toward the table. He shook his head again, more firmly.

"*She* can't reappoint him ambassador to Kronenhof," Aunt Cassandra whispered.

"Should *I* sign something?" Meg whispered on Cassandra's other side.

"Absolutely not!" Aunt Cassandra said. "Don't say anything, either!" She patted the wide-eyed princess's arm. "You've done what you had to; don't give them an inch more."

"I am so grateful to you, Your Imperial Highness," Finn said. "I have never wanted to cause contention, but only seek justice and recognition for my people and our beautiful horses."

"And we are devoted to that cause as well," Genevia said, coming forward to take the emperor's arm.

"No," Cassandra whispered.

Finn realized his mistake at the same moment. "I mean, I do not feel that I have any great injustice to right," he said. "We have had great support from the Crown of Coronam, particularly from Queen Josephine."

"And me!" Meg piped up. She faltered a little under everyone's renewed scrutiny, but Cassandra gave her an encouraging nudge and she stepped forward. "Finding . . . finding out that Finn is my mother's cousin has brought great joy to our family," she said.

"Lovely," Cassandra murmured, lowering her eyes in approval.

"And so have the horses and the Way," Meg went on. "Brought us all great joy. I would do anything for them."

"Stop," Cassandra and Anthea whispered in unison.

Emperor Wilhelm and Genevia positively beamed.

Anthea was afraid to move or say anything. She didn't want to accidentally become betrothed, or be the ambassador to anything. She wanted to go home, and since that wouldn't be possible, she needed to get Meg and Finn out of there, and make sure *they*, at least, got home.

Beloved?

Time to go, Anthea told him.

"Your Imperial Highness," Anthea said. "Your Highnesses." She bowed her head around the room in general, taking in the emperor, Finn, Meg, Fritz, and Wilhelmina. "Might I suggest we now return to the palace? The horses are waiting on the hard pavement, and there are people waiting along the roadway to watch us ride by as well."

"Very well! We are done here!" Emperor Wilhelm announced. Gesturing at the photographer, he said, "I want three copies of everything. As soon as possible." He smiled at Meg. "I want to send copies of them to your parents," he told her.

"Thank you, sire," Meg said. "So kind of you."

"Of course, of course."

But they couldn't leave. It was impossible to leave any place swiftly when you were with an emperor. Everyone had to come through and bow. And bow to Finn and Meg and Fritz and Wilhelmina. And shake hands with the others, or at least nod at them. And they had to be acknowledged; over and over again, Anthea had to bob up and down until her knees ached, and endure the stares and whispers of the ministers as they went by.

"Not much like her mother, is she?" one of them said to his fellow, in her hearing. Both men turned to appreciate Genevia one more time before they returned to the edge of the floor.

Anthea clenched her fists. Outside, Florian let out a whinny, answered by Bluebell. A beat later Leonidas joined in.

Beloved? Let us go back to the palace, Florian suggested. *I do not understand this, and I do not like it.*

I like the stones being regular stones, Bluebell said. *Not slick and terrible. But not the parading or the staring.*

You have all been brave and good, Anthea told them.

"Time to go?" Finn said, taking her arm.

His face was strained. He had never had someone bow to him before this trip, never had people treat him like royalty. And now he had a roomful of people aggressively squeezing his hand and asking him his opinions of taxes and policies. He looked like Florian did when he needed a run.

"Please lead the way, young sire," Genevia said to Finn.

Anthea wanted to snatch her arm away from Finn, to hide forever from the smug approval on her mother's face. Finn was her friend, and she . . . admitted that he was very good looking as well as being . . . very good with horses. But her mother's face made her wish that she and Finn weren't friends. Nevertheless she squared her shoulders, thought of Miss Miniver, and rested her elbow lightly in Finn's hand. He picked up on her cue, and measured his pace so that they were strolling, not fleeing, as they went down the carpeted steps.

They shouldn't have been in front of the emperor, but this was hardly the place to scramble around. Fritz, walking behind his father, made it a very pretty parade indeed as he escorted Meg. They looked like they had just made several grand alliances, and not tricked a handful of children into potentially betraying their families.

The Now King says to tell you that it will be all right, Leonidas said. He sounded as strained as Finn looked.

What is wrong, Leonidas, my darling?

Anthea nearly stumbled down the first step, but Finn held her tight and kept her on her feet. Leonidas . . . something was wrong with him. And the sun had come out from the cloud cover that seemed to filter the light on even the warmest days in Kronenhof. Jilly was standing, like a soldier, in front of the horses, but her eyes were on the other side of the courtyard, where the real soldiers were allowing the people to trickle in and take up places around the edges to look at the horses and the motorcars and the royals.

But that wasn't what was wrong. There was something else. Something that pounded through Anthea's head.

"Can you feel them?" Finn whispered.

"The people?" Anthea whispered back, afraid to say it aloud.

"The horses," Finn said. "Inside . . . it felt like it did at home. Like we were inside the Big House. But it's fading again."

Anthea knew exactly what he meant. It was such a familiar feeling, and there was so much happening, that she had managed to ignore it without realizing. But now it came again. A feeling of horses nearby, not only the ones lined up beside Jilly.

"There is a herd of horses somewhere in this city," Jilly announced in one of her famously loud whispers as they reached for their reins. "It's driving me utterly wild!"

"Something feels funny," Meg said when she reached them.

"Everyone be on their guard," Finn said.

"As opposed to earlier?" Jilly said. "When we were inno-cently out for a stroll, oblivious to our surroundings?"

Finn ignored her. "We must try to talk to the Kronenhofer horses before we go. Andrew wants us to see how many of them would come back with us."

The girls mounted while Finn helped Wilhelm to mount as gracefully as possible. The emperor managed to get into Florian's saddle without completely disgracing himself, but Florian was oozing displeasure so strongly that Anthea was certain that even those without the Way must be able to feel it.

Wilhelm rode out on Florian, and Anthea knew that she would never get used to seeing that. She felt she might be sick, riding behind him, seeing her Florian from this angle. Seeing the emperor looking somehow both smug and awkward at the same—

That strange feeling, of being at the Farm, but not at the Farm, came back in force. Anthea lurched forward in her saddle.

"Are you all right?" Jilly whispered.

"No."

They rode in silence for a minute or two. More people had come to wave and smile, but Anthea looked past them, staring at the buildings and the streets.

She would have plenty of time to explore later, of course.

She could wander the streets and pick up loose gray stones and toss them in the ocean, one at a time.

What do you mean? Bluebell's inner voice was shrill. *We will not stay here! We will go, no matter what The Woman Who Smells of Dead Roses says!*

All the horses heard her. Their heads went up, their nostrils dilated.

"What's going on?" Jilly pulled up Caesar.

In front of them, Florian was prancing in a showy way that Anthea knew meant he was upset. She ignored her cousin in favor of reassuring him, trying to get the stallion to calm.

"What's happening, do you— Marius!" Finn shouted in triumph.

They all turned, and down at the end of an alley they could see him: Marius. And with him, a half dozen of the ghosts of the forest, looking even stranger and more otherworldly in this setting.

"Get out of the way!" Finn shouted at the people gathered to watch the parade.

But by the time a path had been cleared and Leonidas was heading through it, with Anthea and Bluebell on his heels, Marius and the ghosts were gone.

25

PACKING

"WHAT ARE WE GOING to do now?" Finn said, stamping back and forth across Anthea's room.

"You mean now that the emperor is going to Travertine, or because of Marius?"

The one bright spot on the horizon was that they were all going to Travertine. The emperor had announced that he wanted to personally deliver Meg to her father, to show that there was neither ill will nor any "nefarious plot" involved in the princess's long absence from home.

So here was Anthea, packing to go back to Coronam, where she would once again ride Bluebell behind Florian and silently pray for her beloved not to dump the emperor of Kronenhof onto the cobbles. And then when they were done taking photographs and shaking hands, Anthea and Florian and Bluebell would be shipped back to Kronenhof. Forever. Genevia had taken her aside the moment they had returned to the schloss to inform Anthea that, no matter how far from Kronenhof Jilly and Finn were, Genevia would still find a way to make them suffer unless Anthea did exactly as she was told.

"Marius," Finn said.

Anthea actually looked out a window, thinking he had seen the stallion, but she was so caught up in her own nightmare that she couldn't spare the strength for Finn's. She turned away as soon as she saw only empty lawn. Realizing that he wasn't paying attention to her packing, she opened the bureau and tossed an armload of underthings into her trunk.

"We're finally getting out of here," Finn went on, going over to the window himself, "but Marius is missing! And I promised Andrew I would bring some of the Kronenhofer ghosts back home!"

"I've already spoken to Fritz and Wilhelmina *and* Adil," Jilly said as she came in, "and they will watch for Marius. If he so much as shows an ear, they'll herd him onto a ship, with whatever mares wish to join him." She looked around curiously. "Thea, why are you being so picky about packing? Just throw it all in, and we can have it cleaned and pressed when we get home."

"If Marius wouldn't come when I called to him, he's hardly going to allow Prince Fritz to capture him," Finn fretted.

"And there's a reason why they call their horses ghosts, you know!"

"We'll find a way," Anthea said, wishing her voice sounded more enthusiastic. She didn't add that since she would be coming back to Kronenhofer permanently, she would have ample time to tame the ghosts. It was the one bright spot in this mess . . . yet she still wasn't looking forward to it.

"You're both such rays of sunshine I can't stand it," Jilly said. "Don't forget this gown, Thea, it's the best thing you own." Jilly took out the rose pink and gold gown from their first Kronenhofer ball. "I read somewhere that if you roll clothes they don't wrinkle." She spread the gown on the bed.

Anthea closed her eyes and took in a breath. She let it out again, loudly and shakily. When she opened her eyes, Finn was looking at her.

"Headache?" Jilly said, busily rolling the skirt of the gown.

"Anthea, it's going to be all right." He moved in front of her and gently touched her arm. "Once we're back on Coronami soil, we'll be able to spirit you away from your mother and the emperor, I swear it."

Anthea put her hands up over her ears, shaking off Finn's hand in the process. She wanted to shut all this out: Jilly humming as she packed, Finn trying to reassure her. She didn't want to say anything, but she had to, in case they would do something to put themselves in more danger.

She let out another audible breath.

"Thea!" Jilly dropped the rolled gown on the floor. "What has that awful woman done now?"

Anthea screwed up her face, unable to look at her friends. "I'm staying here."

They just looked at her, uncomprehending.

"I mean, I'm going to Coronam, but then I have to come back. With *them*. And Florian and Bluebell. Don't try to hide me or help me. Please."

She clenched her fists and opened her eyes, looking at Finn. "So when I get back I'll find Marius myself. You don't need to worry."

He put out a hand to her again, but she took a step away.

"That's why I'm not packing many clothes. I'll be back in a month. Six weeks. My mother needs to see that I'm leaving some of my best things, so that she won't think I'm going to escape."

"No," Jilly said firmly. "No, no, no!" Her voice became more frantic. "We'll run away, to the northernmost tip of Leana! Or south, to Kadij!"

Anthea shook her head at her cousin. She reached out to hug her, but Jilly was stiff and didn't raise her arms.

"It's her, isn't it?" Finn said gently. He touched Anthea's arm gently, forcing her to look at him. "She's the reason you're so terrified, isn't she?"

Anthea nodded, too miserable to speak.

"She can't blackmail you," Jilly said. "You don't have any

wicked secrets!" She snatched up the pink gown again and began rolling it furiously.

"Jillian! Put that poor gown back in the wardrobe," Aunt Cassandra ordered as she came in. "You're going to ruin it!"

"I am *packing* it," Jilly grated out between clenched teeth. "I am packing all her things! We are not leaving Thea here!"

"Jillian."

All three of them turned to look at Aunt Cassandra, really look at her. She was dressed already for traveling, needing only to pin on her hat to complete her elegant ensemble. But her face was very pale and there were creases around her mouth as though she had been frowning and hadn't had time to reapply her powder.

"Listen to me, all of you," she said in a low intense voice. "We've won this battle, but not the war. The princess is going home, the abducted horses are going home. You, Finn, have been acknowledged as a fellow ruler, and need to get yourself back to Leana to continue to establish that claim." Her eyes went to Anthea. "The next battle will be getting Anthea and all the horses home."

"She told you, didn't she?" Anthea whispered.

"Told you what?" Jilly asked. "Why am I never told things?"

"Yes, Genevia told me," Cassandra said, her eyes locked on Anthea's. She held out her hands, and Anthea took them. They clutched each other's icy fingers.

"I offered to stay as well," Aunt Cassandra said, and Anthea squeezed her fingers even tighter. "But it is not allowed, apparently. Daniel is staying," she added, lifting her eyebrows. "He's sending Deirdre and Belinda Rose back with us, however. Genevia thinks it's because he wants his position as ambassador back, but I think you have an unexpected ally there, Thea. Don't be afraid to seek him out for help."

"Uncle Daniel?" Disbelief took some of the tremor out of Anthea's voice.

"I gather he does not approve of Genevia's behavior, and never had as close a relationship with the emperor as he previously claimed."

"But will he actually help, or merely look disapproving?" Anthea wanted to know.

"Good point," Jilly said.

"Marius," Finn said.

"I'll find him," Anthea said consolingly, putting a hand on his arm now. "He should be safe with the wild horses until I get back."

"No, he's outside!" Finn said, and then he turned and ran out of the room.

Anthea ran after him, with Jilly and Aunt Cassandra following. By the time they reached the lawn behind the schloss there was no sign of any horses, and they could just see Finn disappearing into the distant trees.

"If they go back to those stupid gray rocks, I shall do a murder," Jilly panted.

"Florian!" Anthea yelled, and kept running. *Florian!*

I am coming, Beloved!

Anthea and Jilly didn't bother to go to the stable. By the time they reached the trees, Florian and Leonidas had burst through the flimsy door to meet them.

The girls stopped running so that Anthea could boost Jilly up onto Leonidas, and then Florian bent his knees so that she could hop onto his back sideways, since she was once again wearing a skirt.

As though reading her thoughts, Jilly announced, "I am going to order ten Tenduhai suits as soon as we get to Travertine. Five for you, five for me. This is ridiculous!"

"Agreed," Anthea said, forgetting for a moment that she would not be there.

They soon found Finn, who was standing very still at the edge of a small clearing in the trees. He held up a hand to stop them. On the opposite side of the clearing stood Marius and two wild mares.

"Hello, Marius," Anthea said. "I'm so glad you're all right!"

His ears flicked forward, and the two mares started to slip away.

Marius! Florian commanded. *Stay!*

FLORIAN

Marius's familiar face was framed by two large evergreen trees. And behind him, almost hidden by the trees, stood the unknown mares. Marius flicked his ears at Anthea, and she called out to him.

Precious boy! I'm so glad you're all right!

He crept forward, and the Now King put out a hand and stroked the long white blaze that ran down his nose. His mane was tangled and full of burrs and leaves, but he was in otherwise fine shape, Florian noticed. He had none of the gauntness or the sores of those who had been taken away by The Woman Who Smelled of Dead Roses. That was good.

Are you all right? Florian asked. What happened to you?

Marius hesitated, stepping back. The Now King let him go, but Florian came forward. He made a whuffling noise, reminding

Marius that they had been foals together, and Marius stopped backing up and sighed.

"I'm so sorry," Anthea said aloud. "I'm so sorry about everything that's happened to you. You poor darling. It will get better, I promise!"

Marius felt pleased, but still reluctant. He wasn't hesitating because he was upset: he seemed shy.

These mares, Marius said to the Now King. Their herd is very small now. They do not like men. That Bearded Emperor, he took the stallions away, and they did not come back.

Please, come closer, dear mares, the Now King said, reinforcing it with thoughts of welcome and beckoning. We are friends!

Very slowly two mares stepped out of the trees. They were very fine mares, for not having had a rider to care for them, Florian thought. One was a pale gold color with a nearly white mane and tail, fine boned and delicate. The other was taller than her companion, and a good deal stockier. She had a red mane and tail, but the hair on her body was red and white intermingled, so that she almost appeared to be pink at first. Florian recognized them both from the nighttime meeting.

The Now King carefully stepped forward and held out a hand to each of the mares. They came forward and very tentatively sniffed at his hands. Then they faded back to stand behind Marius again.

Why did you leave? the Now King asked him.

1 . . . I know that I failed you, Marius said. I failed, and the herd stallion and the others were taken. I could not keep up.

It was not your fault! The Now King almost shouted the words. The mares backed up.

I thought I would go to find these others, and bring them to you, Marius said.

You don't need to do anything to apologize, the Now King told him.

Florian found himself nodding, and Beloved Anthea stroked his neck almost painfully hard. He knew that Beloved Anthea agreed with him. They were both glad that the Now King was showing so much love to Marius.

But I wanted to, Marius said. I wanted to do something.

And you have, the Now King said. You have brought these beautiful mares to us! We will take them home with us.

Marius whinnied in amusement. It startled Florian, but the mares joined him.

I am sorry, Marius said a moment later. But no. This is their home. I am not bringing them to you so that they can go to the Last Farm. They must stay here. And I must stay with them.

What?

Florian could not tell if the word had come from the Now King or Beloved Anthea or even himself. Behind him, Caesar moved forward and prodded at him. She Who Was Jilly could not hear what was happening, and was impatient.

They had no herd stallion, Marius said, and there was pride

and wonder radiating from him. Until me. I am now the herd stallion.

"What?" Beloved Anthea said it aloud, and probably too loudly.

The mares sidestepped at the sound of her voice. The golden one started to sidle back toward the shadows of the pine tree. The Now King held out his hands again, and entreated them to stay with wordless pleading.

Constantine is very proud, Marius said finally, picking his way as carefully through the words as he might pick his way down an uneven trail. But even he allows other stallions to stay in the herd.

He is a good herd stallion, Florian agreed.

Despite his pride, Marius said, and Florian flicked his tail uneasily at this criticism.

Marius looked over his shoulder at the two mares.

Their herd stallion was not good, Marius said. He chased away other stallions, or fought them. When That Bearded Emperor came to take some of them, he did not fight, but let the other stallions be taken. He was very strong, and very cruel, and soon there was only him.

He grew old, Marius continued. And died. And left behind only mares, alone.

Oh, that's so terrible! Are they all right? Beloved Anthea blurted out.

They have survived, Marius said.

We are strong, the red mare said.

What is happening? She Who Is Jilly wanted to know. I cannot hear them.

We must have a stallion, the cream-colored mare said. There have been no foals for some time.

There was a long silence. Florian looked at Marius the whole while. He had not seen his longtime herd-mate look this way before. He looked strong, and resolved. He had seemed frightened at first, to speak to the Now King, but that was gone.

The Now King saw it, too.

Can we . . . can we come to visit you? Will you let us help? Do you need another stallion? the Now King offered.

Yes, Marius said. Perhaps another stallion, one without a rider. Augustus or Goliath, perhaps. I will prepare the mares. They have spent their lives running and hiding from men. It will take time.

Thank you, the Now King said. Thank you for being so wonderful.

To Florian's amazement, the Now King was crying.

Marius stepped forward, and the Now King put his arms around Marius's neck in a human embrace. They stood there for a long time. Then the Now King let go, and within an instant, Marius and his mares were gone.

26

THE SECOND PARADE

"HERE WE GO AGAIN," Jilly announced. "Same scratchy blouse and everything."

"But this time's better, because we're home," Anthea said dully.

"No, we aren't," Jilly said, and her voice was sharp. "Home is Last Farm! And we will get you there!"

Anthea didn't have the strength to argue with her. They were vying for space in front of the narrow mirror in their cabin aboard the emperor's personal steamer. They had just endured an unseasonably rough crossing, further aggravated by the presence of the emperor, Genevia, Aunt Deirdre, and Belinda Rose. Anthea had the reminder that she would soon be returning to Kronenhof, forever, dulling her thoughts. And Finn seesawed between elation that they were going home and depression that Marius had stayed behind.

"You both look very pretty," Aunt Cassandra said, coming into the cabin. "Anthea, could you please do something with Arthur." She reached into her handbag and pulled out a small, disgruntled owl. "He's determined to nap in my cabin, and I'm afraid that my little darlings will eat him."

"Sorry," Anthea said, taking Arthur and propping him up on her shoulder.

She felt a pang of guilt. She had hardly paid any attention to him in days, too caught up in her own drama. She had assumed he was sleeping in the hold with the horses, but hadn't thought to check.

"Don't apologize to *me*," Cassandra said, taking up a brush and using it to twirl Anthea's hair into one long, loose curl. "Frankly, everyone should be apologizing to *you*. This whole situation is dreadful. How on earth are we supposed to parade through the streets, smiling and waving, with this hanging over our heads?"

Neither of the girls bothered to answer, because it was the same conversation they had been having the entire journey. There was no solution that any of them could find.

The ship had docked in Travertine early that morning. They would parade off the ship and through the already crowded streets of Travertine, ending on the steps of the Grand Palace, where King Gareth and Queen Josephine would greet them. There would be speeches of friendship and kisses on cheeks. Meg would be delivered into the bosom of her family like a lost lamb returned to a doting shepherd. There would be a formal dinner. A night spent in the palace. And then Anthea would follow her mother and the emperor back through Travertine, back onto the ship, and away.

Anthea leaned forward and breathed on the mirror. In the fogged circle she wrote her name: Anthea Genevia Thornley. Her cousin leaned around her shoulder.

"And Jilly," she said aloud as she wrote it.

"Let's go," Anthea said. "Finn can't do it all himself."

"Aren't you forgetting something?" Jilly sounded shocked.

Anthea turned, putting up a hand to feel that Arthur was still on her shoulder. He was. Her hair was brushed; she was even wearing rouge.

Jilly and Aunt Cassandra were standing side by side, staring at her. In Jilly's hands was Anthea's gray army coat. Anthea turned away.

"I can't wear that," she said as she walked out of the cabin. "I'm not a member of the Horse Brigade. Not anymore."

She went down to the hold and the horses. They would have to bring them up two levels of ramps to the main deck, and then down the gangplank to the dock, and it was going to take every ounce of the Way to keep the horses calm. They had been wild and fretful the entire journey, especially the ones that had been kidnapped.

Finn was already leading the horses out, with saddles on the ones being ridden, and the others as well groomed as they could be. Anthea took the reins of Florian and Leonidas and led them up to the upper deck, tying them to the rail.

It was a beautiful day. The sun was shining brightly, and a fresh, clean breeze was coming down the river from the ocean. The sight of the familiar buildings of Travertine raised Anthea's spirits, only to cast them down again.

Oh, my Beloved, it will be all right. Florian nuzzled her shoulder, the one opposite where Arthur perched. *I will never forsake you.*

I know, my darling.

And I, Dear Anthea, said Leonidas. *Please let me return with you. Please do not leave me behind!*

I don't want to talk about it right now, Anthea said.

The truth was, she didn't want to talk about it ever. She had actually tried to get Finn to demand, as the Now King, that Leonidas stay with the herd, and only Florian and Bluebell return to Kronenhof. But, to her dismay, he had refused. He had told her to take as many horses as she could, for strength and support, which was exactly what she didn't want.

It would just be more lives in danger.

Finn brought up Bluebell and Buttercup, and she tied them alongside the stallions. He looked at her and frowned.

"Where's your coat?"

She shrugged.

"It's too cold to go without," he said. "Do you . . . do you want to borrow mine?"

She turned away, unable to even summon a shrug, and stared at the docks through blurred eyes.

Soon they had their full complement of horses, and Jilly and Aunt Cassandra besides. Cassandra, to everyone's shock, was wearing tailored trousers and insisting upon riding.

"Put this on," she said firmly to Anthea, and handed her the gray coat. "No arguments, young lady!" Her voice was quivering.

"Juniper will cradle you like a baby," Jilly said to her mother.

"I know, I know," Cassandra said. "Andrew said the same thing in his last letter!

"Still, she's the one that you said was very fast. Are we sure I couldn't take one of the poor sickly ones instead?"

"Juniper will make you look better than the poor sickly ones," Jilly said. "Now, why don't we talk about how many letters you and Da have sent each other? Letters I am not allowed to read."

"Oh, pooh," her mother said, waving a hand.

"Are you sure you're ready to ride, ma'am?" Finn asked.

"As though I'm going to get into a motorcar with *Genevia Cross*," Cassandra said. "The very thought is repulsive!"

"How delightful," Genevia said coldly, coming up to them.

Anthea put on her coat, the rustling of her clothes loud in the silence, and nobody spoke or looked each other in the eyes.

Meg, bouncing on her toes at the prospect of finally seeing her parents again, checked on Blossom's saddle, and then they were ready. The princess was insisting on riding her favorite mare, and even though Blossom was still recovering, the mare was determined to carry her chosen rider in the parade.

The emperor and Meg would lead, and Finn would come behind them, riding Leonidas and leading Constantine. The herd stallion had a purple saddle blanket to cover the worst of his half-healed wounds. After them would come Anthea on Bluebell, Jilly on Caesar, and Aunt Cassandra on Juniper. Anthea would have Brutus on a long lead, and Jilly would have Campanula, while Aunt Cassandra occupied herself with staying in the saddle. After that, one of the Crown's own motorcars would drive Genevia and Wilhelmina, Deirdre and Belinda Rose, with a troop of Kronenhofer soldiers going in front to clear the way, and an honor guard of Coronami soldiers bringing up the rear.

Thus they made their way, in solemn procession, along the waterfront and up the Mile. The wide street ran from the river to the Crown Palace, rising gently all the way. People holding flowers and little Coronami flags lined both sides, and Anthea forced herself to smile and nod as they made their progress toward the palace.

She could have held Brutus's lead and Bluebell's reins in one hand and waved with the other, but she frankly didn't want to. For most of her life she had dreamed about traveling up the Mile in the entourage of a member of the royal family. And now here she was, with a rose on her lapel, following in the wake of a princess she considered a friend, and looking forward to embracing the queen . . . But it was like a peach with a rotten pit: beautiful on the outside, but one bite revealed the spoiled inner part.

"Keep that smile in place," Jilly hissed. "*Somebody* has to smile!"

Anthea jerked the corners of her mouth up, but looked around a little more carefully at Jilly's words. Words that she had heard very clearly, because beyond the sounds of the soldiers' boots on the cobbles, the purr of the motorcar, and the *clop clop* of the horses' hooves, there was nothing. No one was cheering. No one was calling out to them from the sides of the road. Everyone was just watching the dreaded horses move past, silently.

Meg was waving and blowing kisses, her smile bright and unfeigned. Some of the children holding flowers tried to run out and give them to her, one of their beloved princesses, but their mothers held them back, clearly afraid of the horse that the princess dared to ride. It seemed that the queen's efforts to chase away the stigma of disease and death that the Crown had laid upon horses for generations had not been successful, not with the Dag outbreak so recent.

Anthea closed her eyes. She couldn't do this. She couldn't make it up the Mile, not like this. This wasn't how her long-dreamed-of triumphal parade to the Crown Palace was supposed to be. She saw Bluebell's ears flicker back as the mare sensed her distress. A moment later Bluebell spoke to her.

Caesar says that She Who Is Jilly says that she is going to fix this. She Who Is Jilly has spoken to the New Meg. They have a plan; just follow along.

And open your eyes!

Anthea opened her eyes. Mostly because she was worried about what plan Jilly might have.

But it was Meg who moved first. Waving with both hands, her reins draped across her lap, the princess guided Blossom with her knees over to one side of the road and leaned toward a girl with a bunch of daisies in her arms. Holding the pommel easily with one hand, Meg reached out and took the bouquet from the girl, and Anthea heard the princess say something about Blossom, indicating her mare and then the flowers. The girl had backed away as soon as the bouquet was out of her hands, but she was grinning broadly.

Now Jilly swooped to the other side of the road, having handed Campanula's lead to her mother. Aunt Cassandra, to Anthea's eyes, looked even more terrified, but to someone who didn't know her, she was every inch the coolly collected Rose Maiden. Jilly took a bouquet from a child, thanking her extravagantly.

We shall also have flowers, Bluebell announced. *Brutus can walk by himself. He is a stallion grown.*

Anthea barely had time to toss the lead line across Brutus's back before Bluebell trotted over to a young woman about Anthea's age with a brightly colored bouquet. The girl eagerly held them out as soon as Anthea met her eye.

"Thank you," Anthea said uncertainly, bending over to scoop up the flowers. "How nice."

"Horses brought us medicine," chirped the young boy standing beside the girl. They both beamed.

"Oh. Oh!"

Anthea had all but forgotten the brigade's attempts to bring medicine to those stricken by the Dag. She hadn't thought they had gone as far as Travertine, but perhaps these people had come from outside the city.

As they moved back and forth, waving more naturally, smiling, taking in flowers until they overflowed their arms and all three girls had to guide their horses with their legs and just hold on to their bouquets, the crowd began to relax as well. Some people still looked guarded, if not actually frightened, but others seemed curious and a few, who Anthea noticed were dressed in more rustic clothes, looked excited. She guessed that they had seen horses before, passing messages or medicines.

Jilly took the crown of flowers someone had handed her and put them on Finn's head, causing a ripple of amusement to run ahead of them through the assembly. Finn laughed and adjusted the crown to a more rakish angle, and Anthea saw a girl in the crowd let out an obvious sigh.

Anthea tucked flowers behind her ears, stuck them in Bluebell's mane, and gave a gardenia to Arthur, who held it in his beak to the delight of the children watching. She placed some of the more neatly tied bouquets across her aunt's lap, to free up her hands. By the time they had topped the rise and were almost to the Crown Palace, the crowd was sending up little cheers, calling out for Princess Margaret, and Anthea had even heard a few cries of "The Horse Brigade!" and one piping child's voice asking, "Are those the Horse Maidens?"

Anthea's smile was real now. The horses had their heads up, their ears forward, and their hooves were lifting and striking the cobbles in a sprightly rhythm. Anthea laughed when Arthur suddenly buffeted the side of her head with his wings and dropped his gardenia into her lap.

Then he bit her, hard on the earlobe. She clamped her legs on Bluebell's sides, involuntarily, hissing at the pain. Bluebell stopped short, tossing up her head.

Together, Anthea and Bluebell watched as something small and dark sailed out of the crowd just outside the palace gates and landed in the middle of the Kronenhofer soldiers.

The grenade exploded just as Anthea realized what it was.

FLOWERS AND FIRE

ANTHEA DROPPED HER ARMLOAD of flowers. All around her, people were screaming, but she could hear them only dimly after the ear-shattering sound of the grenade exploding. For a second, nothing else moved save for the falling flowers and the falling soldiers.

Her eyes went immediately to Florian, who was closer to the explosion. He was on his feet, Emperor Wilhelm on his back. Anthea started to call out, to tell him to come away, to come to her, when Florian reared up and dumped the emperor onto the hard cobbles of the street.

"Florian, no!"

Florian spun away from the fallen man, pivoting on his hind legs. He butted against Blossom's shoulder, hard, with his chest, turning the mare as well. Florian surged past Blossom, toward the crowd gathered on the right side of the road. They were screaming, scattering, their faces terrified.

But it wasn't because of the grenade. When she heard the second gunshot, Anthea realized that the noise of the first one had largely been covered by the sound of Florian neighing and throwing down his rider, plus the leftover ringing in her ears.

"Shooters! On the right!" Anthea shouted as she had been taught.

But the mares hadn't been taught battle tactics. They were trained to take a defensive stance if threatened, to run if alone or huddle together if in their herd. They were panicking just as much as the humans.

Get me to Florian, Anthea ordered Bluebell, who was dancing in place, unsure of what to do.

More gunshots came. The crowd was running in all directions, screaming, but Bluebell made it to Florian's side in two strides. Anthea had her feet out of the stirrups and was on Florian's back in a single leap.

The stirrups were too long, the saddle too big, but it didn't matter. This was Florian. He would never let her fall.

She barely had to touch the reins for Florian to move into the front of the formation, with the others falling into place behind. They put the mares, with Meg on Blossom, in the middle. Leonidas moved onto the right, Caesar on the left. Jilly tersely gave orders to Meg as she unclipped the leads from the extra horses. Meg, who had never been battle trained, nodded, lips tight, while Anthea scanned the buildings around them.

There was no sign of a shooter; the gunshots had stopped after three? Four? Anthea wasn't entirely sure. Now there was just screaming and running and . . .

No. Wait.

From her vantage point atop Florian's tall back, Anthea saw a movement that was wrong. Someone was moving against the crowd, fighting their way *toward* the street, not away. Anthea could only see dark hair and a gray coat, and then the person gave a leap and something flew from their hand.

"Grenade!" Finn shouted.

The grenade seemed to fall incredibly slowly. Anthea thought she could see the arc of it in the air, like a colorless rainbow that ended in the back of the open motorcar where Aunt Deirdre sat with Prince Adil, Belinda Rose between them.

"For the Crown!" the man shouted in Coronami, and then another shot rang out, this time from the gun of a Kronen-hofer soldier, and the man dropped like a marionette with its strings cut.

Anthea saw this from the corner of her eye because she had already wheeled Florian around and charged at the car. She clamped his sides with her legs as tightly as she could and leaned far away from the saddle toward the car.

Belinda Rose was screaming, her face red, and Aunt

Deirdre was shoving her out of the car. They both tumbled to the ground alongside Genevia, who was already out of the car, standing to the side.

But Princess Wilhelmina saw Anthea coming and threw her arms up like a child asking to be carried. Anthea grabbed the much taller young woman under her arms and dragged her across the long back of the car as Florian kept running. Wilhelmina's skirt had caught on something in the car, Anthea realized, and that was why the princess had not gotten out before. There was a ripping sound, and the princess's full weight almost dragged Anthea out of the saddle. But since she was now clear of the car, Anthea let Wilhelmina fall.

Florian finally slowed and allowed her to turn him as she was righting herself with an effort. The motorcar sprang into the air and then fell back on its wheels with a crash, the doors wrenching open, and the glass of the windscreen shattering.

Florian stumbled to a complete halt, and Anthea, unbalanced in the ill-fitted saddle, swung down to the ground beside Wilhelmina. She had a tight grip on the reins, which dragged Florian's head down and to the side awkwardly, but she didn't care. She knelt by the Kronenhofer princess, afraid to look at anything else.

"I'm fine," Wilhelmina gasped. She was holding her hip, and her gown was ruined, but she waved Anthea away. "Go! See what's happening!"

Anthea staggered toward the burning motorcar, a dim

thought in her head about the gasoline in the tank being more dangerous. Florian came with her, bracing her. Cassandra was on the ground, Finn kneeling beside her while Leonidas looked on. Jilly raced past Anthea on Caesar.

"Mother!" Jilly cried out, and threw herself from Caesar's back onto Aunt Cassandra, sobbing.

There were soldiers everywhere, and black military motor-cars arriving. Anthea looked around at the palace, vaguely wondering if anyone from the royal family had seen what had happened. Would they come to help, or go inside to be safe? She didn't know the protocol. But she couldn't see anything except for the soldiers. So many soldiers!

One of them stepped in front of Anthea. He had a rifle, and it was pointed at her.

"What are you doing?" she asked him.

"Step away from the animal," he said.

"What?"

"You're under arrest for the attempted assassination of Emperor Wilhelm," the soldier said. "Now step away from your animal or I will shoot it."

Anthea put her hands up. Florian, reins dangling, didn't move. What were they going to do with him? With any of the horses?

"We didn't ... we didn't do this," Anthea gasped out. "How could we?"

"Be quiet!"

Beloved?

It will be all right, my darling. But you must tell me: Are any of the horses hurt? Where is the New Meg? Where is Finn?

All are well— Beloved!

Anthea could hear it, too, a voice cutting above the chaos. A woman's voice, powerful, commanding, but ragged and damaged from screaming.

"Everyone move! It's going to blow!"

"The gasoline," Anthea whispered.

The soldier looked at her in horror. He let the point of his rifle sink down.

Beloved!

Anthea needed no further encouraging. She had hold of Florian's saddle and was halfway into it before the soldier could open his mouth to order her to stop.

"Get down!" she ordered him, and then she kicked Florian into motion.

He bolted away from it all: the motorcar, the soldiers, the screaming, and the sound of a third, and far worse, explosion. Heat and noise slammed into Anthea's back just seconds after Florian shot down a side street. It rocked her forward, and she nearly went headfirst over Florian's neck. His hooves slipped on the cobbles, but he managed to stay on his feet and keep running, and she stayed on his back where she belonged.

He would never let her fall.

Anthea's ears were more than ringing now. They felt like

they had wads of cotton shoved in them, and she worried that she was permanently deafened. Fortunately, the Way didn't require one to have ears.

Take us east, she told Florian, trusting his sense of direction far more than her own. *Three streets from the palace. And north one block. And tell the others!*

But what is this place?

Uncle Daniel's house, Anthea told him.

Will they look for us there?

Yes, but we have nowhere else to go, she countered. *Tell Con and the others!*

They needed a place to hide, to rest, to check for injuries. Then they would need to find a way to get to the docks and hire a ship. One that could take them north along the coast, to Leana.

"I want to go home," Anthea whispered as they clattered through the streets.

She was surprised to find tears streaming down her face. Her ears had stopped ringing, but she wasn't sure what she was hearing. There was a booming . . . more explosions? Had the fire spread?

I have told Leonidas to bring the Now King and meet us at the uncle's house, Beloved.

Good. Tell the others, Anthea said.

Dear Anthea, Bluebell said. *I have Campanula and Brutus. Juniper has the Good Aunt, the mother of She Who Is Jilly.*

Bravo! You're wonderful! Anthea said, fighting down her guilt at leaving everyone behind.

Beloved! That man would have shot you! Florian reminded her in outrage.

Anthea didn't answer. More tears came, blinding her. She clung to Florian's back and let him have his head, weaving through the streets and the scatterings of people, the parked motorcars, and the ox carts. They turned onto a familiar street, lined with trees, the houses built of the same pale stone as the palace.

Through her tears, Anthea saw the familiar façade of the house where she had lived with Uncle Daniel, Aunt Deirdre, and her cousins. It looked just the same, though the shutters were tightly closed, making the house seem like it was asleep. Anthea guided Florian toward it, bringing him to a slow halt beneath a linden tree. They both sighed heavily.

The others will soon find us, Florian said.

I know, Anthea fretted. *But what then?*

She wasn't really waiting for an answer, though. Her attention had been caught by a motorcar just ahead of them. It was parked in the side lane between Uncle Daniel's house and the Denvilles', a family whose identical twin sons were always being suspended from school for various pranks. Anthea had once heard Lady Denville tell Aunt Deirdre that she had made her husband swear not to buy a motorcar until the twins were adults, because she just knew they would get into a horrible accident.

So what were the Denvilles doing with a brand-new motor-car? In fact, it was a Pritienne, just like Princess Wilhelmina's new car.

Beloved? Someone is coming!

It was a man on foot. He came pelting around the corner facing them, stopped for just a second as though confused about where he was, then ran for the Priti. He was wearing a gray coat, much like Anthea's own, but she saw at once that the buttons were wrong and the lapels far too wide to be army issue.

As he twisted to get into the seat his eye fell on Anthea and Florian. All the color drained from his face. Anthea felt the blood rush into hers, however. He turned away, started the car, and shot up the street.

Follow him! Anthea ordered.

Who is he?

He's the man who shot at Emperor Wilhelm . . . and you! But he's Kronenhofer!

Anthea had recognized him the moment they had locked eyes. He was one of Wilhelm's personal guards, the one who had told her about the ghosts in the forest. The last time she had seen him had been a few days before they left Kronenhof, and she had assumed that he had stayed at the schloss.

But here he was in Travertine, wearing a coat that looked almost, but not quite, like a Coronami officer's coat, throwing grenades, shooting guns, and shouting death to the emperor.

The speedy little car racketed through the streets of Travertine, and Florian stayed right behind it. This was no straight and carefully swept racecourse, but a cobbled street in a city that Anthea knew, and the soldier did not. The street soon forked, causing the soldier to hesitate and then spin the wheel hard to the left. Anthea, as soon as she saw the car begin to turn, sent Florian in that direction. And when he went left again at the next cross street, Anthea began to laugh.

Florian, my darling, tell the others. This is where we are going. Tell Constantine, and Leonidas. Tell Caesar and the mares. Is Holly here? Is Domitian? Tell every horse you can find to go here!

In her mind, Anthea pictured the place where the soldier was going. He didn't have a choice, not unless he got out of the car. The streets in this part of Travertine curved around and met at Princess Jennet's Park. Anthea knew these streets well, had traveled them twice a day the entire time she had lived in Travertine. On three sides of the park were grand houses, grander even than Uncle Daniel's.

And on the fourth side of Princess Jennet's Park stood Miss Miniver's Rose Academy.

They are coming, Beloved!

Excellent!

Anthea bent low on his neck, doing her best to cling to the large saddle. The stirrups were too long, and it was hurting her to have her legs dangling. She pulled them out of the stirrups and tucked them up in the position they should be in, holding tight with her knees.

The soldier turned right down the street that made a circle around the park. Anthea yanked Florian's reins so that he went the other way. It almost made her laugh, thinking how the soldier would assume he had outraced her when he didn't see Florian galloping behind his car. The iron fence encircling the park was covered in climbing roses, making it opaque, and the gates were all locked, Anthea noticed as they clattered past. No doubt to encourage the park's usual gathering of children and their nurses to attend the parade instead.

Constantine is here, Florian told her.

Tell him to go left, with Leonidas and the Now King, Anthea instructed. *And Brutus. Tell the mares to go right, and find us.*

Yes, Beloved!

Anthea was almost giddy with laughter. Perhaps it was shock. Perhaps it was because she was once more on Florian's back, and they were running, running, running, as they loved to do. Perhaps it was the joy of being able to do something, anything. They would catch this man, and then . . . Well, there was no need to think beyond simply catching him.

Florian ran even faster, slipping a little on the cobbles as they came around the corner. But he, too, felt the joy of the chase, and as they turned again and saw the motorcar heading toward them, he whinnied in triumph.

The brakes screeched, and the motorcar came to a halt directly in front of the gates of Miss Miniver's Rose Academy. Anthea sat up and let Florian go to meet the car at a trot.

The soldier revved the engine and started to turn, but braked hard when a trio of stallions came racing around the corner. Constantine was in the lead with Leonidas and Brutus at his heels.

Finn was still riding Leonidas, but it was clear that the enraged Constantine was in command. He strode right up to the side of the motorcar, and Anthea thought the herd stallion might trample right over the hapless soldier.

The clattering of hooves behind Anthea announced the arrival of the others. Bluebell came at once to Anthea's side, with Aunt Cassandra clinging to her back, pale but determined. Jilly, on Caesar, positioned herself on Anthea's other side. Then Meg and Blossom were there, beyond Jilly. They had made a wall on either side of the motorcar.

The soldier cut the engine. He looked like he might run, or cry.

"What are you doing here?" Finn demanded, urging Leonidas forward. "You didn't sail with us!"

"He's the one who threw the grenade," Anthea said, moving Florian up on the other side so that he was right against the side of the motorcar. "And shot at the emperor." She looked at him steadily. "Why did you try to kill your own emperor?"

"I—I did not," the man said in heavily accented Coronami. "I—I did not. It was Coronami. Coronami start a war. Kill our emperor."

"*You* tried to kill your own emperor," Finn said.

The sound of engines drowned out whatever protest the man might have tried. Great black military motorcars pulled up behind both sets of horses. Coronami soldiers—real Coronami soldiers—spilled out of the cars with their guns drawn. It was like watching a magic act: there were so many soldiers that Anthea could not figure out how they had all fit into the cars. They immediately pointed their guns at the horses, at the riders, and finally at the soldier in the car. There was at least one gun per target, and they froze into position, ready to shoot any person or horse that moved.

And then a sleek silver car arrived and disgorged its passengers: King Gareth. Queen Josephine. Princess Annabel. Princess Wilhelmina. Emperor Wilhelm.

Genevia, who was the only one smiling.

"This is an outrage!" Emperor Wilhelm said at once. "I come to Coronam to deliver your princess home safe and sound, and I am attacked! Attacked by Coronami soldiers, by your horses, by a brother king!" He pointed wildly around, at his own soldier, at the horses, and at Finn. "This goes far beyond firing on my ship," he went on, turning on King Gareth, face red with outrage. "This means war!"

Princess Wilhelmina gasped, as did Princess Annabel. Aunt Cassandra looked grim, and rather like she would have gasped if the others hadn't.

Anthea looked over the heads of the soldiers, the

assembled royals, and met Finn's eye. He nodded. Anthea sat up very straight in Florian's saddle, lifted her chin, and made a small gesture with one hand.

Following her lead, Finn threw back his shoulders and lifted his chin. Anthea caught herself smiling approval, realized how much she probably looked like either her aunt Cassandra or, at worst, Genevia, and schooled her expression back to one of grim resolve.

"King Gareth," Finn said formally. "Although you do not formally recognize Leana as a sovereign nation, and myself as its ruler, I swear on my name as a magTaran of Leana that all Emperor Wilhelm has said is false. This man"—he pointed to the soldier, who was either sweating or crying—"is one of Emperor Wilhelm's personal guards, and with my own eyes I saw him throw a grenade and fire a gun near, but not at, his own emperor. It is clear that there is a conspiracy afoot, but I am convinced that you are not behind it, and can assure you that I am not!"

"Father," Meg cried out then, and Queen Josephine broke through the line of soldiers and reached up to take hold of her daughter's hands. Meg smiled tremulously at her mother, and then went back to her father. "Father, you know very well that I was kidnapped by Kronenhofer soldiers under the command of that woman!" She pulled a hand free of her mother to point at Genevia. "And after I was freed, I was tricked into some bizarre stunt to make it look like I'm betrothed to Crown Prince Fritz!"

"Are we really going to stand here listening to these children's accusations?" Genevia interrupted. "You all know that my own daughter has been turned against me by the exiles up north. And now you see how she has infected them all!"

"Brilliant, Genevia," said a cool, elegant voice. "I don't know which is more disappointing: that you never went on the stage, or that you choose to use your talents to such wicked ends."

Beloved? Are you all right? Who is this woman?

"Miss Miniver," Anthea whispered, turning to Florian.

28

THE THIRD PARADE

EVERYONE TURNED TO WATCH the arrival of a tall, impeccably dressed woman in cream satin. Her white hair was adorned with jade combs carved with roses, and she was leaning on the arm of Anthea's uncle Daniel. Anthea was hard-pressed to determine which of these newcomers caused her greater shock.

Then Uncle Daniel gently released Miss Miniver's arm and came right up to Florian, and Anthea couldn't stop her jaw from dropping. His face was almost gray with relief. He actually reached up and took hold of Anthea's hands, reins and all.

"Are you hurt?" he demanded in a low voice.

"Am I . . . what are you . . . what's happening?" Anthea croaked.

He's touching me! Florian complained.

Anthea gently took her hands out of her uncle's grasp. She moved Florian to the side a little. Uncle Daniel, seeming to understand, or perhaps remembering his revulsion for the horses, moved aside as well.

"Are you all right?" Uncle Daniel asked again.

"You weren't with us," Wilhelmina said. "We brought your wife and daughter . . . how did you get here?"

"I took passage on a small Kadiji boat that left moments after the imperial yacht," Daniel said. He glared at Wilhelm. "The captain is a cousin of Prince Adil who came to the schloss with some personal messages. Since the prince wasn't there, the captain told me what he had seen: members of the Imperial Guard getting on a merchant ship bound for Travertine. Why, he wondered, would the guards leave for Coronam the day before the emperor? And not in uniform?"

"Your Majesty," he said to King Gareth. "I swear to you, my wife and I only went to Kronenhof to visit old friends. We had no political agenda whatsoever."

King Gareth's eyes narrowed, and Uncle Daniel had the grace to blush.

"Very well, it doesn't hurt to keep on good terms with royalty," Uncle Daniel admitted. "But that was all! Just to remind the emperor of our previous friendship.

"My half sister was not there on a social visit, however." He gave Genevia a scathing look, and she lifted her chin in response. "She and Wilhelm have been meeting for years and have plots within plots: abductions, false alliances, and now this attempt to start a war with a fake assassination!"

"That's not even the right kind of coat," Aunt Cassandra said with a flip of her hand at the failed assassin. "Wrong buttons, wrong shade of wool."

"And those lapels," Jilly put in.

"Very good, Cassandra," Miss Miniver said. "And may I say, you look surprisingly well sitting upon that beast?"

"Oh, thank you," Aunt Cassandra said modestly. "I don't have the Way, you know, but there is still rather a thrill to it all."

"I will give you a gold crown to say that to Da's face," Jilly said out of the side of her mouth.

"Ladies don't gamble," Aunt Cassandra chided her.

"Or mumble," Miss Miniver added.

"Now what?" Anthea said. "Now what do we do?" She looked at King Gareth. "You do believe us, don't you? Please, sire! Please believe us!"

"I know my father," Wilhelmina said. She drew a deep breath. "And if you won't believe Finn and Anthea, then believe me, King Gareth."

Tall and icy and severe as she always was, when not behind the wheel of a motorcar, the princess looked around and caught the eyes of the king and queen, Cassandra, Daniel, and then King Gareth again.

"My father and Anthea's mother are two schemers who never should have been allowed in the same room," Wilhelmina said. "I was certain, when that ship was blown to pieces months ago, that it was a calculated attempt to start a war. My father had to have had someone in Coronam helping him."

"Genevia," Daniel said grimly.

Wilhelmina nodded.

"She engineered a war *and* a plague?" Jilly said, sounding hysterical. "What is *wrong* with her?" She turned to Genevia. "What is wrong with you?"

"She wanted to be queen," Anthea said. "And when that didn't work—"

"She settled for empress," Wilhelmina said bitterly.

"Must we stand in the street and discuss this?" Genevia said with distaste.

"I have to say I agree," Miss Miniver said. "This isn't a matter that needs to be laid out in the open air."

"No, by gad, it isn't," King Gareth said. He glared around at everyone equally. "What a fine pickle! Assassinations! False treaties! Hostages!"

He suddenly seemed to notice the soldiers still pointing guns at the riders and the horses. Including the horse his own youngest daughter was sitting on.

"What the devil?" he raged at his men. "All of you, guns on the emperor and this one," he said, indicating Genevia.

"Not the girls! Fools!" He took a steadying breath. "Get these two back into a car and take them to the pier." He leveled a look at Emperor Wilhelm from under bushy brows. "You won't have your war, sir, but if you set foot in my country again, you'll see some fireworks, if you know what I mean!" He turned to Princess Wilhelmina. "And you? What to do with you?"

"I have never been to Travertine, Your Majesty," Wilhelmina said with a slight bow. "Perhaps I could stay for a while? To ensure my father's good behavior?"

"Very nice, excellent," King Gareth said. "I like you."

"And if I might also volunteer?" Prince Adil spoke up. "I have a great wish to discover if what I have read of Coronam is also true."

King Gareth looked baffled by the Kadiji prince wearing a Kronenhofer uniform.

"Who the devil—"

"Prince Adil has been a hostage in Kronenhof for years," Finn said. "If it isn't in Coronam's best interests, Leana would be proud to give him sanctuary until he can be returned to his own home."

King Gareth's eyes narrowed. "All our allies are welcome at the palace," he said. Finn nodded regally, and Adil bowed.

The soldiers leaped into action then. They arrested the hapless assassin and gently but firmly put Wilhelm and Genevia into separate cars. Genevia paused with one foot on the running board.

"Anthea, dear," she said.

"Don't you speak to her," Aunt Cassandra said hotly.

"How *dare* you?" Queen Josephine said at the same time.

"Genevia, just go," Miss Miniver said, sounding tired. "And take that rose off your lapel. I have never been so appalled!"

"Quite," Queen Josephine said, and held out a hand to take it from Genevia.

For the first time, Genevia Cross looked genuinely abashed. Her fingers shook as she unpinned the gold brooch and dropped it into the queen's hand. Without another word she got into the car and was driven away.

When the three cars were out of sight, Meg suddenly let out a little sob. Her parents flew into action, and had her in their arms before she had completely dismounted. Her sister Annabel joined in and soon all four were hugging and crying.

Anthea got down from Florian's back and helped her aunt Cassandra onto the ground. Miss Miniver came over to shake both of their hands, but then Finn was at her elbow. When she turned to look at him, he gave her an awkward hug but backed off at once to make room for Uncle Daniel, who kissed her rather formally on the cheek, and then stepped aside for the queen, who swept Anthea and then Jilly into her embrace.

"Oh, my darling girls! My Horse Maidens!" The queen was laughing and crying. "You did it! You're wonderful!"

"Indeed," King Gareth said, and to Anthea's shock, he

first pumped her hand the way he would have a man's, and then leaned over to kiss her cheek as well. "Horse Maidens! Very fine!"

"Well, we couldn't have done it without Finn," Anthea mumbled.

"You know, Kronenhof *and* Kadij recognize his claim to Leana," Jilly said, and then gasped as her mother elbowed her sharply in the ribs.

There was a long silence.

"We have much to discuss," King Gareth said after a minute. "But first, we have our people to reassure. All is quiet here, but on the Mile . . ."

"I can lend you my motorcar," Miss Miniver offered. "It has an open top and isn't quite so . . . warlike." She looked at the remaining army car with an arched eyebrow.

"Ah, thank you!" King Gareth said. "Just the thing!"

"I'll send it out," Miss Miniver said. "I am too old for such excitement. But I expect you to call on me . . . all of you," she said, fixing the queen, Aunt Cassandra, Anthea, and even Jilly with a stern eye. "And tell me everything." She looked at Uncle Daniel. "Escort me into my house. I have a driver, but perhaps it would look best to have you drive the royal family back to the palace."

"Very good, ma'am," Uncle Daniel said, and meekly followed her through the iron gates.

"Now," Queen Josephine said briskly. "Gareth, you and

Her Imperial Highness can ride with Daniel. And Cassandra, too, you look too done in to get back on Bluebell."

Aunt Cassandra agreed demurely.

"You rode Bluebell?" a man's voice broke in. "Cassie? You were on a horse and I missed it?"

They all turned to see Uncle Andrew riding up. He wore a smart gray Coronami uniform with a knotted Leanan horse-shoe embroidered on the breast, and his hair and beard were disconcertingly well trimmed.

"Oh, *Andrew*," Cassandra murmured. And then she called out, "Yes, I did! I did ride a horse! Then I fell off one and got back on another!" She let out a girlish giggle.

Anthea and Jilly and Finn all gaped at her. Prince Adil laughed softly. Jilly closed her mouth and then opened it again to say something, but Anthea grabbed her arm.

Andrew swung down out of the saddle and came over to them. "I'm so sorry I'm late! Caillin MacRennie and I were waiting at the palace, and we had to round up the horses you abandoned first."

He said this last line very severely, looking at Jilly and Finn.

"Are they all right?" Finn asked anxiously.

Andrew softened. "Well, yes. Other than the shock of see-ing Caillin MacRennie cry when he saw Brutus!"

"Oh, that dear man," Queen Josephine murmured.

"And you did have bigger things to do, I see." Andrew

286 Jessica Day George

glanced about and then Jilly wrapped her arms around him, making him laugh as he hugged her and kissed her head. "Ah, my Jills!"

"We've had the *worst* time," Jilly said into his coat. "You should have come to Kronenhof!"

"You handled yourselves admirably," Josephine said. "We couldn't have hoped for a better outcome!"

"We did our best," Finn said.

"You did us all proud, from what I can tell," Andrew said, gesturing around at Meg, the horses, the assembly. "Your Majesty," he added with a twinkle.

He let go of Jilly to shake Finn's hand, which turned into a rough hug and ended with a lot of masculine back patting. Anthea and Jilly shared an eye roll. Anthea tentatively stepped forward, longing to hug her reassuringly solid uncle herself, but it was Aunt Cassandra who got there next.

"Oh, Andrew! I rode a horse," she sobbed all over his coat, clutching at the lapels as though they were holding her upright. "Me! And you, you raised two wonderful girls! And Finn! And that sweet boy became a doctor! And it was just awful! But also exciting! And Genevia, I tried to tell you she was up to no good! Why didn't you listen to me then?"

"I'm sorry, I'm sorry," Andrew murmured. He bent to kiss her head, realized that she was wearing a large flowered hat, bent lower to kiss her cheek, saw his daughter and niece and nearly a dozen other people watching, and turned a dull red before straightening.

Tears were pouring down Jilly's face, and she ran to throw her arms around both her parents. Anthea felt Josephine's hand on her shoulder.

"I never would have thought," she murmured.

"It's so sweet," Meg whispered, and then turned to explain to the baffled Wilhelmina and Adil.

"My girls," Andrew murmured. He looked up and met Anthea's eyes. He let go of Jilly and held out a hand to her. "All my girls!"

Eyes flooding with tears, Anthea ran into the embrace. Anthea thought she had never been so warm, so happy, so safe. So loved.

Beloved? Florian sounded reproachful.

This is second to finding you again, my love, she assured him.

Humans need other humans, Bluebell said wisely. *I can't understand it, myself. Loud, awful things!*

That made Anthea laugh, and gave them a chance to separate and mop up their faces with handkerchiefs. A chastened Uncle Daniel arrived with Miss Miniver's motorcar, and Josephine began to arrange everything.

"Everyone will be wondering if we're dead," she fussed. "We had better show them that it's quite the opposite!"

"Even more reason for a parade now," King Gareth agreed.

He couldn't stop reaching out to touch Meg's shoulder or hair, clearly so moved to have her returned. Anthea thought that Genevia might have vastly misjudged the king's feelings about having only daughters.

"I'll ride Bluebell, if she doesn't mind," the queen went on. "The rest of you mount your usual horses, I suppose. Does Constantine need to be led, or shall he make his own way, as your brother king?" she asked Finn with a twinkle.

"I'd better lead him," Finn said. "He doesn't like crowds. Or motorcars." Finn smiled. "Or people."

"I've met men like that," Queen Josephine said, and she cut her eyes at her husband.

"I beg your pardon, ma'am?" he huffed at her, but a faint smile appeared beneath his mustache.

"It looks like a lot has happened here as well," Jilly said under her breath to Anthea. "The Woman Who Smells of Dead Roses is going to find it a lot harder to make mischief next time."

Anthea could only nod, bearing up under the sudden blow her cousin's words had inadvertently given her. She found that she was shaking, and Finn had to boost her into Florian's saddle. He adjusted the stirrups while she sat like a lump. She didn't know how long she sat there, staring at the park without really seeing it, but suddenly they were all moving into formation behind Miss Miniver's glossy green motorcar, the very one that Anthea had learned to drive.

Beloved? Florian asked anxiously. *Are you all right?*

"Are you all right?" Finn echoed unintentionally. He was

riding beside her, Constantine on his other side and pushing a little ahead of the others.

"I'm fine. I'm just . . ."

And then tears were coursing down her face for the second time. Florian tried to stop, but Anthea spurred him on, not wanting the others, who were all behind her and Finn, or ahead in the car, to see.

But Josephine was there in an instant. Anthea suspected that Bluebell had told her, because the mare came right up so that she and Florian were walking in tandem and Anthea's knee was bumping against the queen's.

"My dear girl," Queen Josephine said, putting a hand on Anthea's shoulder, "what is it? I mean, beyond the obvious."

"She's going to kill them," Anthea said dully, too exhausted to lie. "Somehow. She's going to kill Finn. And Jilly. Probably Adil, just because he was kind to us. And any horses she can. Marius. The ghosts of the forest.

"All I had to do was let Wilhelm ride Florian, but I couldn't . . . he wouldn't . . ."

I am sorry I threw off the Bearded Emperor, Florian said, not at all remorseful. *But he is not a good rider. He did not get back on.*

The Mother of Jilly got back on, Bluebell noted. *And she is afraid of us!*

Anthea burst out laughing. Through sobs she told Finn and Josephine what Florian had said.

"Very true, Florian," Josephine said. She tossed a look and a headshake over her shoulder at Jilly and Meg, who were trying to move up to see what was happening.

"But here's the thing, Thea dear," the queen said. "Your mother has sought all her life to have power. And she has failed, again and again. And for the last time. After this, do you really think that the emperor will marry her and make her his co-ruler?

"She's driven away anyone who cared about her: her family, her friends—if she ever had them," Josephine went on. "Her name will be taken off the rolls of the Rose Maidens," the queen said fiercely. "And they will all know, and every Maiden will know, about her treason." She looked over at Anthea. "And do you really think that anyone would raise a hand to harm you? Or Finn? Or Jilly?" She smiled, and Anthea felt a little sob escape again. "Who would dare to try?"

I will protect you, Florian said. *I will never forsake you!*

I know, my love, I know. But it's not me I'm worried about.

Another voice broke into Anthea's thoughts through the Way. She almost didn't recognize it, there was so little of the usual rage, which had been replaced by pride.

I would die before I let anyone harm our herd, Florian's Anthea, Constantine said. *No man shall harm our riders, not Caesar's Jilly, and never the Now King.*

I—I, of course—thank you, she replied, startled.

All will be well, Florian said.

All will be well, chorused the other horses. *And soon we will go home.*

Soon, Beloved, Florian promised. *Home to Last Farm.*

Yes, Anthea said, and managed to dry the last of her tears on her sleeve. *We will go home.*

They moved through the streets, the palace rising ahead of them now, in stately procession. Cheers rose up as the motorcar bearing the king came into view. More cheers, and cries of astonishment, were raised as people saw Queen Josephine sitting proudly on Bluebell's back.

The queen moved up to ride alongside the car, and King Gareth held out a hand to her. Miss Miniver would have beamed in approval, could she have seen how easy Josephine made it look to hold hands with her husband when she was riding a horse and he was sitting in a car.

Behind Anthea, Meg and Jilly smiled and waved. The horses tossed their heads and pranced, and Constantine stepped out like a soldier marching in triumph.

Finn reached over and took Anthea's hand. Florian and Leonidas were moving in perfect step, and it was the most natural thing in the world for Anthea and Finn to hold hands as they moved toward the gates of the palace.

"Soon we will go home," Finn said.

"And all will be well," Anthea whispered.

ACKNOWLEDGMENTS

I would love to give everyone involved in this series a pony of their very own, but since horses are a lot of work, maybe just a puppy. But books are also a lot of work, and third books in a trilogy particularly, so at the very least I need to thank so many people for all they've done!

A huge thank-you to everyone at Bloomsbury who believed in the Horse Brigade from day one, when it was almost a non-magical World War I cavalry horse story. The amazing Beth Eller, in particular, has been a huge supporter of this series, and I will be eternally grateful to her!

And this book benefited from not one, but two sets of editorial eyes, so a huge round of applause and many hugs go out to Mary Kate Castellani and Claire Stetzer, whose excellent guidance put the shine on this book. Love you, ladies!

And speaking of shine, I have been blessed over the years with many gorgeous covers, but this one became a favorite the moment I saw the first sketch. Thank you, Kevin Keele, for perfectly capturing Florian and his Beloved Anthea!

All my gratitude and love, of course, to Amy Jameson: Best of Agents, Finest of Friends! Thank you for all your hard work, not to mention the emotional support and the delicious lunches—I mean, strategy sessions! You are amazing!

And to my family, and not just my husband, who brings me treats in my writing cave, or my brilliant and beautiful children (who really should bring me more treats in my writing cave) . . . but to my parents (who wouldn't buy me a pony but always secretly face out my books in bookstores), all the way down to the tiniest nephews and niece . . . this one's for you! I love you all!